Kern County Library

1. Books may be kept until last due date on card in this pocket.

2. A fine will be charged on each book which is not returned by date due.

3. All injuries to books beyond reasonable wear and all losses shall be made good to the satisfaction of the librarian.

4. Each borrower is held responsible for all books borrowed by him and for all fines accruing on same.

DEMCO

BIRTHDAY, DEATHDAY

by Hugh Pentecost

A RED BADGE NOVEL OF SUSPENSE

DODD, MEAD & COMPANY, NEW YORK

ISBN: 0-396-06523-6
Library of Congress Catalog Card Number: 71-38524
Printed in the United States of America
by Vail-Ballou Press, Inc., Binghamton, N.Y.

Part One

CHAPTER 1

The State Department man was a very cold fish. He looked like a Madison Avenue advertising executive—Brooks Brothers suit with a vest, crew-cut prematurely gray hair. He wore a wedding ring on his left hand, which suggested that somewhere in his life there was some unexpected warmth or sentimentality. He talked about human life and death as though the people involved were numbers in a computer, or toy soldiers with nameplates on them. Perhaps you develop the habit when you're accustomed to dealing with the war casualties in Indochina—numbers, not humans.

"We have to believe," he said, "that the man we are after has absolutely no concern for his own survival. He will attempt to find a way to confront General Chang and kill him. After that nothing else will matter to him."

We were in Pierre Chambrun's office on the second floor of the Hotel Beaumont in New York. Chambrun is my boss. I am the public relations man for the hotel. The Beaumont is New York's top luxury hotel, although Chambrun would question that description. Top luxury hotel in the world, would have been his designation. He had been its resident manager for twenty years. He didn't think of it as a hotel. He had often referred to it as "a way of life."

The office reflected Chambrun's cosmopolitan tastes. It was a large room with no office equipment visible except for the three telephones on Chambrun's carved Florentine desk. The floor was covered by a magnificent Oriental rug. Facing the desk on the far wall was a Picasso, the artist's blue period, a personal gift. The furniture was substantial, comfortable. On a teakwood sideboard was a Turkish coffee maker that was constantly in operation. After two cups of Colombian coffee at breakfast, Chambrun drank his Turkish brew the rest of the day.

Chambrun is a short, dark man, black eyes buried deep in heavy pouches—eyes that can show compassion and understanding, or can be as cold and hard as a hanging judge's. That morning he was the hanging judge, slumped down in his big desk chair, eyes narrowed against the smoke from his Egyptian cigarette.

"You are proposing to turn my hotel into a shooting gallery, Mr. Foster," he said.

"I propose to keep it from becoming a shooting gallery," Foster said. "Roy Worthington Foster" his official card, lying on Chambrun's desk, proclaimed him to be. Like I said, a cold, cold fish.

"There must be a hundred other places where you could hide your Chinese Napoleon," Chambrun said.

"He can't be hidden," Foster said. "His mission is public. He is here to appear at the United Nations. He has to be seen, interviewed by the press and by television and radio reporters. He has to be kept safe or the international repercussions will be at a disaster level."

"We make strange friends in this day and age," Chambrun said. "But why here? Why must he be kept safe here?"

Foster wasn't trying to butter up Chambrun when he said: "He would be expected to stay at the best hotel in the city. Other foreign diplomats he will want to confer with, unofficially, live at the Beaumont. For him to stay anywhere else would be illogical."

"And if I say 'No'?"

Foster's face was expressionless. "The United States Government wants him here," he said. "The President himself has made matters clear to Mr. Battles, the hotel's owner. You cannot say 'No,' Mr. Chambrun."

Chambrun put out his cigarette and lit a fresh one. I know him so well. He was seething with anger but it didn't show. Mr. George Battles, the Beaumont's owner, lives on the French Riviera, presumably counting his endless supply of money. He is rumored to be the richest man in the world. To him the Beaumont is a sort of prestige toy. To the best of my knowledge he hasn't been in the place for fifteen years. He rarely puts any pressure on Chambrun and when he does it is usually over some trivial matter: a rowdy friend whom Chambrun would normally kick out on his ear, a lady whose morals are questionable, credit for someone who doesn't rate credit. He would, I guessed, have been much flattered by a personal request from the President of the United States. Foster was right. Chambrun couldn't say 'No.'

Chambrun's mouth was compressed into a thin line. "Details," he said.

Roy Worthington Foster took a small notebook out of an inside pocket. "General Chang's party arrives at Kennedy Airport tomorrow at 3 P.M. There are twenty-two members in the mission—a valet; two secretaries, female; one secretary, male; thirteen subofficials, three married couples and seven single males; four male bodyguards, two to a room on each side of General Chang's suite; in addition there are four FBI agents and two CIA men. All these people must be installed in adjoining rooms on the same floor."

"Impossible," Chambrun said. "We don't have any such vacancies."

"Make it possible," Foster said.

I thought Chambrun would explode, but he didn't. His eyes were two glittering dots in their deep pouches.

"Your own security staff—I presume you have one—will cooperate with the CIA man who will be in overall command of the forces protecting General Chang," Foster said.

"And your psychotic assassin who doesn't care if he dies or not?"

Foster put his notebook back in his pocket. For the first time I thought I detected some sort of personal emotion. "His name," he said, "is Neil Drury. If you watch any of the late movies on television—"

"I do not," Chambrun said.

"I've seen him," I said. "A very good young character man." A forgotten memory stirred. "Don't I recall that his father was in your department, Mr. Foster? He was abducted and murdered by Communist revolutionaries—in Argentina, wasn't it?"

"In Argentina, five years ago," Foster said. He took a carefully folded handkerchief from his breast pocket and touched his lips with it. "Walter Drury was shot by a firing squad. His wife and daughter were brutalized, raped, murdered—in Drury's presence before he died." Foster touched his mouth again.

Chambrun's eyes widened. "And General Chang was the impresario of that horror?"

"Young radicals in South America were schooled and indoctrinated by trained terrorists from other Communist countries, notably Cuba and Red China. Chang is known to have been operating in that field."

"So we roll out a red carpet for him," Chambrun said.

"So help me God—"

"We have no choice," Foster said. "Neil Drury, quite understandably, wanted revenge. He demanded redress through diplomatic channels, without success. Then he tried to handle the matter himself. Chang was back in Peking. Neil Drury went to Hong Kong, dreaming that he could somehow get into Red China and find his way to Chang. It was an absurd notion. Drury was well known as an actor, his face familiar. Chang's men were waiting for him and he just did escape from Hong Kong with his life, with Red hatchet men and our agents on his trail. We have been looking for him ever since."

"So he walks in here, his face familiar, and Chang's boys write him off," Chambrun said.

Foster was looking intently at the toe of one well-polished shoe. "He won't be readily recognized," he said. "We understand he has undergone extensive cosmetic surgery. I could sit next to him in your Trapeze Bar, Mr. Chambrun, and not know him."

"You would have known him before the surgery?"

A nerve twitched in Foster's cheek. The man did have feelings. "I was Drury's department boss at the time he and his family were massacred. I sent him to his death. I knew Neil well."

"But now you are protecting General Chang!"

"My job."

"Lucky you," Chambrun said.

"And your job, Mr. Chambrun," Foster said. He blotted at the little beads of sweat on his upper lip.

Chambrun is not a man to cry over his bad luck or moan about his outrages. I knew that morning how much he resented being put behind that particular eight ball. The only perfect day for him is one when nothing whatever disturbs the Beaumont's Swiss-watch operation. Because he is a perfectionist, I guess there has never been such a day, but everything is relative. Mr. Roy Worthington Foster left Chambrun that morning with a massive headache. To begin with, the need for adjoining space for some twenty-eight people was a hotel man's nightmare. The demand for accommodations at the Beaumont is endless; people make reservations weeks in advance. We have what we call "house seats," a phrase borrowed from show business. We keep two suites and a half dozen rooms available for emergencies. The Beaumont is a sort of headquarters for foreign diplomats; we get unexpected requests to house important people. Important people in all walks of life think of us as a home away from home. Our reservations manager, Mr. Atterbury, juggles these house seats as people come and go. Last minute requests from old patrons can usually be filled, but twenty-eight Chinese diplomats, bodyguards, secretaries, plus FBI and CIA agents, in adjoining rooms, was impossible. Knowing Chambrun, I knew it would be managed. Accomplishing the impossible is his specialty.

The threat of some kind of violence in his hotel was far more disconcerting to Chambrun than trying to juggle room assignments. In my years with the Great Man there have been more than a few violences and Chambrun has shown a special talent for dealing with crime, but he takes violence in the hotel as a personal affront. It's as if an attack has been intended on him. I should like to go on record as saying that he is a pretty tough counterpuncher.

"We have to be ready for this invasion by noon tomorrow, Mark," Chambrun said to me when Foster had left us. "Atterbury and I will do the juggling of the rooms. It's going to involve some very special pleading. I have a job for you."

"Get ready for the army from the press who will be in the General's wake," I said, guessing brightly.

"That's ordinary routine," he said. "I want you to locate Neil Drury."

I just stared at him. The Chinese secret agents, the State Department, the FBI and the CIA had been looking for Neil Drury without success. Mark Haskell, public relations director of the Beaumont, didn't seem like a very probable hero in this department.

"Where would you suggest I start looking?" I asked. "He doesn't look like himself. He's managed to hide from the best intelligence services of two countries. You're not serious."

"Deadly serious," Chambrun said. "Try thinking a little, friend."

"But I—"

"You're not a detective," Chambrun said. "I know. But you are a hotel man, and I have sometimes suspected that you have a pretty sound knowledge of people and what to expect from them."

"I'm flattered. I'll remind you of that when the day comes you decide to fire me."

"I haven't time for jokes," Chambrun said. He was already asking the switchboard to connect him with Atterbury. He held his hand over the receiver. "I don't know Neil Drury, but it's not hard to make some shrewd guesses about him." Atterbury evidently came on and Chambrun ordered him to report on the double. He put down the phone. "Our Mr. Foster didn't suggest it, so I wonder if something fairly obvious has occurred to him and his FBI and CIA geniuses."

"Nothing obvious has occurred to me," I said.

"Neil Drury is not your paid professional political assassin. Foster implied that, when he told us Drury wasn't concerned with his personal safety—after he gets to Chang. This is a man eaten away with the need for personal revenge. It isn't going to be good enough for him to put a bullet through the General's head from some sniper's post. He needs to face him; he needs to have Chang feel some of the terror Drury's family felt before they were slaughtered; he wants to hear Chang plead for mercy before he cuts out his heart. So he has got to get to Chang long enough to relish such a moment."

"The General must know that," I said.

Chambrun nodded. "Knows it and has surrounded himself with personal protectors, along with skilled help from Uncle Sam. On the face of it one would have to think that Drury hasn't got a chance. Unless—" Chambrun's eyes narrowed.

"Unless what?"

"Drury must have a plan. It will involve making himself completely familiar with all the routines we set up to protect the General. He'll need a few days to study and check every precaution we take. Don't you see, Mark, there's only one obvious place to look for Drury."

"Here in the hotel!"

"Where else?" Chambrun got up and crossed over to his Turkish coffee maker. "As of this morning there were a thousand and fourteen guests in the hotel. We have chapter and verse on ninety percent of them. That leaves a hundred and two people we don't know as old customers, though some of them have stayed here before. Some of them are women. I doubt if there are more than fifteen or twenty men we can't wipe off the list of possibilities. Check them all, down to the brand of toothpaste they use, Mark. Check with people in their towns, their businesses, their families. The minute you come up with one who doesn't phase out, let me know at once."

"Right."

"That's really routine your staff can handle, Mark. The main problem is to identify Drury. Dig back into his history. He can change his face, but if he is six feet two he can't shrink, and if he's five feet seven he can't grow. Find out, if you can, who his friends were before he went into hiding behind his new face, his women, his habits. Does he smoke? Does he drink in moderation or to excess? What kind of liquor does he drink? What are his eating habits? Hobbies— does he read, go to movies? I want the most detailed rundown on him you can provide, Mark."

"Foster could have supplied you with a lot of those answers," I said.

Chambrun leaned back in his desk chair, the tips of his square fingers pressed together. "Interesting character, Foster," he said. "He has a job to do for his department—protect General Chang—and he'll do it to the best of his ability. Personally he would like to protect Drury. He sweats a little when he thinks about it. He'll close up like a clam if we ask him for help, because he'll be afraid it might get back to his superiors that he has two aims. When and if the going gets tough he might be useful to us, but not yet."

"You want to help Drury?" I asked.

His eyes were hidden by their heavy lids. "I don't want a killing in my hotel," he said.

CHAPTER 2

Guests of the Beaumont would be surprised if they knew how complete is the hotel's information on them. There is a good deal more than name, address, and credit references.

There is a card for each guest, and there is a code used which is most revealing. The code letter A means the subject is an alcoholic; W on a man's card means he is a woman chaser, possibly a customer for the expensive call girls who, from time to time, frequent the Trapeze Bar; M on a woman's card means she is a manhunter; O arbitrarily stands for "over his head," meaning that particular customer can't afford the Beaumont's prices and shouldn't be allowed to get in too deep; MX on a married man's card means he's double-crossing his wife, and WX means the wife is playing around. The small letter "d" means diplomatic connections. If there is special information it is written in the form of a memo on the card, and if this information is not to be public knowledge in the front office, the card is marked with Chambrun's initials, meaning that the Great Man has special knowledge about the guest in his private file.

The two very efficient girls in my office, down the hall from Chambrun's, set to work checking the cards on our one thousand and fourteen guests. It was not as difficult a job as that number suggests. They should have eliminated all but a handful in a couple of hours. I set about the job of trying to find out what I could about Neil Drury.

The early phases of it were not too difficult. Actors' Equity, the performers' union, put me onto one David Tolliver, who had been Drury's agent. Tolliver turned out to be quite willing to help. He had been fond of Drury, and Drury had been a profitable client until tragedy had removed him from the acting field. Tolliver's office was only a few blocks down Madison Avenue from the Beaumont, and I caught him there shortly after lunch.

Tolliver was a happy fat man wearing a loud checked sports jacket that made him look like an overweight wrestler.

"I'd do anything in the world I could to help Neil," he

told me. He was slightly flushed, which indicated there had been several martinis at lunch.

"He's walking into an almost certain death trap," I said. I explained that there were Chang's personal bodyguards, the FBI, the CIA, and Jerry Dodd, our extremely efficient security officer at the Beaumont, along with his staff. If he tried to get to Chang, he'd be chopped down—with regret except by Chang's men. "I want to find a way to identify him when he shows so that we can warn him off, perhaps save his life."

Tolliver lit a long, thin cigar. "Nothing is going to stop him from trying," he said. "He's been trying for five years."

"Do you know who the doctor was who performed the operation to change his face?"

"No." Tolliver swung around in his chair so that he was looking out the window, away from me. I wondered about him.

"That doctor could save us a great deal of work at a time when there is so little time," I said. "He could tell us what Drury looks like."

"I don't know who the doctor was," Tolliver said. "I don't know where the operation was performed—here, in Europe, in the Far East." He turned his chair back to me and I decided he was telling the truth. "Neil was one of my best clients. He worked steadily in films, television, and on Broadway. He was making a film in Hollywood when his family was wiped out. He phoned me to say he was walking out on his contract and flying to South America. Nobody could blame him. I heard from him again only once, about a month later. He phoned me from somewhere here in the city. There would be money coming in for him, residuals from films and quite a few TV commercials he had done. Ordinarily I held that money for him and we settled up about twice a year. He asked me to deposit anything that came in, large or small, to his account in the Irving Trust. I wanted to see him, talk to him. He refused. He sounded like a stranger. That was the last time I ever talked to him; almost five years ago." Tolliver knocked the ash off his cigar. "I have a file on him—pictures, his resumé. There are also news clips on the South American horror. If you'd care to see them—?"

"Bless you," I said.

There were several pictures of Drury in different poses, and a half dozen stills from films and Broadway plays. He was not a romantic type, but even in a photograph you sensed enormous energy. I was reminded a little of the late John Garfield, though Drury was evidently a somewhat bigger man. On the back of one of the photographs was his resumé. It listed his unions; his height, five foot, eleven; his weight, one hundred sixty-five; color of hair, black; color of eyes, gray blue. He was graduated from Columbia University in 1958 and had done graduate work in theater at Brandeis after that. It didn't give his age, but he would now have to be in his late thirties, I thought. There was a long list of acting credits. He would have been what Tolliver would have called, "a valuable property."

Along with the pictures were some slightly faded newspaper clippings. They told the story of the Drury tragedy. The first one was a news flash. Walter Drury, ambassador to Argentina, his wife and daughter, had been kidnapped by revolutionaries and were being held hostage against the release of some four hundred political prisoners and a hundred thousand dollars in ransom money. There was a photograph of the Drurys at some official function. Walter Drury was a solid-looking man of dignity and charm. Mrs. Drury was a handsome, well-groomed woman in her early fifties, I guessed.

Joanne Drury was a heartbreakingly beautiful young girl in her late teens or early twenties. Separately, there was a picture of Neil Drury, "well-known actor of stage and screen." It seemed that two members of Walter Drury's staff, two young men, were also abducted.

There followed clippings of efforts being made to negotiate with the kidnappers, none of them successful. The Argentine government "refused to be blackmailed." Nobody really believed that the Drury family would be harmed. After all, they were American citizens!

Then the story broke. One of the two staff members who had been abducted, a Peter Williams, staggered into a suburb outside the capitol. He had been blinded. His story was so incredible that people thought at first he was in some kind of delirium. The Drurys were dead. The other staff member was dead.

"They held us there, made us watch," Williams told reporters. "There were perhaps a hundred men in the kidnap force. Mrs. Drury and Joanne were stripped in front of us all—beaten—and then they were assaulted by dozens of men. I guess you would call it a gang rape. All the time Mr. Drury was screaming at them that he would pay anything, do anything. Mrs. Drury and Joanne were dead before it was over. Then Mr. Drury and George Raynor were ripped to pieces by machine-gun fire. I thought I would be the next and the last. The leader approached me. He seemed to be Chinese or perhaps Mongolian. He was a big, powerful man, bigger than most Chinese I have ever met. 'You will go back to your imperialist masters and tell them what you have seen. Tell them there will be new hostages taken unless they meet our terms.' And then he took a knife out of his belt and—and he gouged out my eyes. Somebody was ordered to guide me back to town."

I could feel the sweat in the palms of my hands.

"Pretty story," Tolliver said.

I didn't answer. The next clipping, obviously selected by Tolliver because of his personal interest, described Neil Drury's arrival in South America. Peter Williams' big, powerful Chinese had been tentatively identified as General Chang, a Red Chinese expert in terror. Neil had demanded reprisals and been refused. He had flown back to Washington and made an attempt to see the President. The President had sent him a letter of regret, but had been "unable" to see him. The State Department had listened to him, promised nothing.

The final clipping was dated some two years later. It told of Neil Drury's escape from Chang's men in Hong Kong, where he had obviously gone to attempt to gain personal revenge for the murder of his family. The original story was rehashed. The only thing new was a statement from General Chang, denying that he had ever been in South America or had anything to do with the "regrettable" deaths of the Drurys.

I put the clippings down on Tolliver's desk. My mouth was dry as cotton. Tolliver looked at me with something like sympathy.

"You can understand, I guess, why Neil has gone off his rocker," he said.

"He has to be stopped for his own sake," I said. "So since we can't put a face to him, I need to ask a hundred questions about his habits, his appetites, his physical and personal eccentricities."

"Probably changed, like his face," Tolliver said. "Neil is a trained actor. He would easily make a whole new character for himself."

"Just the same—"

"There is someone much better equipped than I am to answer the kind of questions you want to ask," Tolliver said.

"Oh?"

"Peter Williams."

"The man who was blinded?"

Tolliver nodded. "He lives here in New York, somewhere down in the Village. I think I have his address and phone." He reached for an indexed book on his desk. "Grove Street," he said. He wrote down an address and telephone number on a slip of paper and handed it to me. "Williams went to school and college with Neil. That's how he happened to get a job with Walter Drury. He was like a member of the family in his teen-age years. He knows all there is to know about Neil's personal life. They shared an apartment here in town when they were both getting launched."

"He's still blind?"

"You read the clipping," Tolliver said. " 'Gouged out my eyes.' You don't grow new ones, Mr. Haskell."

He lived in a ground-floor apartment, two small rooms, kitchenette, and bath. It had a small square of garden at the back, and he was sitting there, his face turned up to the sun, when I first saw him. When I rang his doorbell he called out to me from the garden to come in.

The living room into which I walked was bare, no pictures on the walls, no books. There was, however, what looked like a very expensive sound system: record player, AM–FM radio, and tape recorder. There were two large, comfortable, leather chairs, and a small plain table near the door to the kitchenette. Through the open top half of a Dutch door I could see him in the garden.

He was blond—almost bleached blond from much exposure to sun. His face was tanned a copper brown. It was a handsome face; high cheekbones, straight nose, a wide, rather too-firm mouth. He wore black glasses over his eyes. They were rather unusual glasses, more like goggles. They fitted tight to his face so there was no way you could glimpse what lay behind them. When he stood up and held out his hand I saw that his body was slim, lithe, well conditioned.

"Mr. Haskell?" he asked. His voice was deep, rather pleasant.

I had called him from Tolliver's office for an appointment, and given him a brief notion of why I wanted to see him. He'd been immediately ready to help. He gestured me to a wicker armchair with a comfortable cushion in it. He sat down again and his right hand closed over a blackthorn stick with a crooked handle that was hooked over the arm of his chair.

"I'm grateful to you for seeing me, Mr. Williams," I said.

He wasn't for small talk, it seemed. "Tell me about Neil," he said. The black glasses were focused directly on me. I had to remind myself that he wasn't seeing me through those opaque lenses.

I laid it on the line for him. General Chang was making a highly publicized visit to New York. He was to stay at the Beaumont where I worked. The State Department, the FBI, and the CIA were convinced Neil Drury would make an attempt to get at him. We in the hotel, along with the others, were ordered to protect the General. Chambrun wanted to get to Drury before he walked into almost certain destruction.

"He knows Neil?" Peter Williams asked.

"No."

"But he sympathizes with him—with his cause?"

"Maybe," I said. "His chief aim is to keep his hotel from being turned into a slaughter house."

"You're honest, anyway," Williams said.

"I've just finished reading a batch of clippings David Tolliver has," I said, "which include your account of things at the time. Personally I'd like to see Drury get to Chang."

"Oh, he'll get to him unless he's warned off," Williams said.

"You think he'll get through the professional cordon that will be set up around the General?" I asked.

The thin, straight mouth moved in a bitter smile. "He'll be allowed to get through," Williams said.

"Allowed?"

"Chang knows he will come. Chang will let him through. Neil will be allowed to think he's being very clever and Chang's men will chop him down. There will be polite expressions of regret over the death of a madman."

That possibility hadn't occurred to me and it made me feel a little sick.

"Chang is no fool," Williams said. "He has a very complex and highly sophisticated mind. He knows he has a chance to rid himself of a danger that's been hanging over his head for five years. Neil can't win. He will certainly try, and he will certainly lose."

"Then we have to spot him before he moves," I said. "Chambrun thinks he will take a day or two to scout out the lay of the land, which means he'll probably check into the hotel. How do we identify him?"

I had been fiddling with a pack of cigarettes.

"Smoke if you like," Williams said. Then, as if he could see the surprise on my face: "I could hear you playing with the edge of the cellophane on that package. I can also smell the tobacco. I used to be a three-pack-a-day man myself. But after this—" He raised his right hand toward the black glasses. "When you can't see, you have to sharpen all your other senses. Smoking interfered with my sense of smell." He chuckled. "If I met you again in a strange place and you didn't speak I would still know you, Haskell. I would smell you." He laughed. "I'm not telling you something 'your best friend wouldn't tell you.' Everybody has his special smell. That's why a dog can follow his master's trail. He doesn't see the footprints. He follows a scent."

"Thanks for the reassurance," I said. "Are you trying to tell me that if you came close to Neil Drury you would know him—by his smell?"

He frowned. "I'm not sure. I haven't seen Neil since—since this happened to me. I'd know anyone I've met in the last four years, since this began to work for me. Neil—I don't know. I don't think so. But there is something I would know. I'd know the sound of his voice, no matter how carefully he disguised it."

"Could you?" I must have sounded doubtful.

"In the old days, when we were both starting out after college, we shared an apartment in town."

"Tolliver told me that."

"Neil got his first acting jobs in radio. He was very usable because he could change voices. He was expert at three or four accents: British, Spanish, Italian, Scandinavian. I used to cue him when he was working on those accents. I know all his tricks of speech and inflection. No matter what he has taken on for his new face, his new identity, I'd recognize his voice."

"We'd better move you into the hotel," I said.

"If you like."

"Then you will help?"

"Of course." His mouth tightened. "I love that guy."

"You can probably tell us a lot of other things about him," I said. "Does he smoke?"

"Chain smoker."

"Drink?"

"Vodka. Vodka martinis on the rocks, vodka and tonic, vodka straight."

"Will you come back to the hotel with me? Will you talk to Chambrun? Will you help us?"

"Give me ten minutes to pack some duds," Williams said.

CHAPTER 3

Williams moved around his apartment as easily as I would. While he packed some shirts, underthings, shaving kit, an extra pair of slacks and a light tweed jacket, I phoned the hotel and asked for Chambrun. Instead I got Miss Ruysdale, his fabulous secretary. The boss was in consultation with the CIA man who was to command the defense of General Chang. He couldn't be interrupted.

"But he's been screaming for you for the last hour," Miss Ruysdale said.

"I've come up with a gold mine," I said. "Neil Drury's best friend in the old days. I'm bringing him to the hotel to stay—and help."

"I'm sure you'll get a gold star," Miss Ruysdale said, in her cool, crisp voice.

I got her to switch me to Atterbury, the reservation clerk, who sounded a little hysterical. "Are you out of your mind?" he asked me. "We've just finished arranging to house twenty-eight unexpected guests and you want a room for a friend! There isn't a place to pack in a sardine."

"Then he'll have to share my place with me," I said.

I explained to Williams that I had an apartment on the second floor, next to my office. It consisted of a sitting room, bedroom, and a small kitchen and bath.

"The couch in the living room opens up into a reasonably comfortable bed," I said.

"Actually, if you don't mind, it may be for the best," he said. "I'll be closer to what's going on if I'm with you."

"It's fine with me," I said.

We locked his apartment and went out on the street where I spotted a taxi and hailed it. The way he handled himself was extraordinary. He didn't walk with his stick out in front of him, tapping his way along. Only when we hit the pavement did he reveal his infirmity. He let his left hand rest lightly on my arm.

In the cab he leaned back, relaxed, the black glasses focused on the back of the driver's head.

"If we're going to be living together, Mark, we'd better get over the initial embarrassments," he said.

"Embarrassments?"

"You're wondering why I don't carry a white cane, why I don't have a dog."

He was right; I had been wondering.

"I can't bear to call attention to myself," he said. "I've worked for five years to avoid that 'blind man's look.' I can learn a new environment very quickly. I try not to appear publicly in a place until I've had a chance to study it thoroughly. I've wanted a dog, mostly for company." His mouth tightened. "I can sense things, quickly, acutely. The minute I used a white cane or a dog I would—I would smell pity." He turned his head slightly. "I smell it now."

"Sorry," I said. "I'll get over it."

"You're also wondering why I wear these goggle-type

glasses," he said. "If you got a sidewise glimpse of what's back of them, you wouldn't have much appetite for dinner." He leaned back again, relaxed. "With your help I'll learn your apartment and the areas in the hotel where I'll be most likely to run across Neil—the bars, restaurants. It won't take me long."

We arrived at the Beaumont and went in. I bypassed the desk. I would sign him in later. On the way to the elevator, Williams' hand resting on my arm, I saw Johnny Thacker, the day bell captain. Johnny is a skinny blond with a shrewd gamin face.

"This is Mr. Williams, Johnny," I said. I made a little gesture toward my eyes. "He'll be sharing my place for a few days. Make yourself useful if he needs you."

"Right," Johnny said. "You're lucky to have a friend here, Mr. Williams. We're coming apart at the seams. They're even turning away people who had reservations."

In my living room Williams put down his bag. He stood there, turning his head from side to side. "Tell me about it, Mark."

I told him where the furniture was: the couch, the two comfortable armchairs, the sideboard, the desk, the extra small chairs, the bookcase, even the paintings and photographs on the wall. He began to move slowly around, not feeling with his stick. In five minutes he could walk to every piece of furniture, not awkward. We went through the same routines in my bedroom. We located the two phones, one by my bed, one on the living-room desk. We went through the small kitchen where he learned the location of the stove, the icebox, the china cabinet, the rack from which my few pots and pans hung, the shelves where I kept my staples and condiments. In the bathroom he checked out the shower, the medicine cabinet, the linen closet. His concentration was so intense it hurt.

Will you be all right if I leave you for a while?" I asked him. "I have to check in with Chambrun."

"I'll be fine, Mark. I look forward to meeting your Mr. Chambrun. He's something of a legend."

"He's a pretty great guy. If I'm going to be longer than half or three-quarters of an hour I'll phone you. If you need anything special send for Johnny Thacker, Mr. Williams."

"It's Peter, I hope," he said, smiling.

"That's fine with me—Peter."

"I'll get unpacked," he said.

Someone should write a book about Miss Ruysdale, Chambrun's secretary. She's on the tall side, with dark red hair, thick, cut short and worn like a duck-tailed cap. Her face, the bone structure, the straight nose, the high forehead, the wide mouth are almost classically beautiful. She is, I know, all woman but she affects an almost male severity in her dress and manner. Chambrun would want his secretary to be attractive, but not some chick who would have all the male staff making perpetual passes at her, interfering with his needs. I suspect Miss Betsy Ruysdale might be the most interesting woman I know, but I have never been able to penetrate beyond her efficient, friendly-but-impersonal, office manner. Everyone concedes that there must be a man hidden away somewhere in Miss Ruysdale's life. God forbid he should know it, but I have wondered if that man might not be Chambrun himself. You'd never know it by his manner. He neuters her by calling her 'Ruysdale,' never Betsy or Miss Ruysdale. And she—well, she makes herself indispensable by anticipating everything he needs, night or day. I have been in his office a hundred times when he's said, "I'll get Ruysdale to hunt up that document for you." He'd press the button on his desk and Miss Ruysdale would appear, document in hand, before he'd asked for it. It was as if she was tuned in on a private wave length.

Miss Ruysdale was at her desk in the outer office when I got there. She gave me her special little impersonal smile, one dark eyebrow raised quizzically.

"You find a crevice for your gold mine?" she asked.

"My living-room couch," I said. "His name is Peter Williams. He's blind, by the way."

"The sole survivor of the Drury massacre," she said. You're never very far ahead of Miss Ruysdale. She reached for a stack of papers on her desk. "I'd prepared you a set of clippings on the Drury business. But if you've got hold of Peter Williams, you won't need them."

"Thanks for thinking of me, ma'am," I said.

"I was thinking of Mr. Chambrun," she said.

"Alas!"

Her eyes twinkled. "There is not time for flirtations, Haskell. Here is a Xeroxed copy of a floor plan of the rooms set aside for General Chang and company. Twelfth floor. Two suites, ten doubles, seven single—both sides of the corridor."

"You must have had to move some people around," I said, studying the plan.

"The Great Man is exhausted from being charming," she said. "He's also burned by the necessity of putting up people who had reservations at some of the competition—the Plaza, the St. Regis." She smiled faintly. "He is also being burned at the moment by the bland assumption of Mr. George Wexler that he can give the orders."

"Wexler?"

"The CIA man who is to be generalissimo of the defense forces." She nodded toward the closed door of Chambrun's office. "You're to go in. If he barks at you, know that he really wants to bite Mr. Wexler. Good luck."

George Wexler looked like an amiable, pipe-smoking, college professor. He was sitting in the armchair across the desk from Chambrun, whose eyes were two narrow slits in their pouches. Jerry Dodd, the Beaumont's security officer—we don't call him "house detective"—was standing by a far window, his back to the other two men. I guessed he was struggling with laughter.

Wexler turned his shaggy, rumpled head my way, pipe dangling between his front teeth. He took the pipe away and smiled as if he was delighted to see me.

"Where the hell have you been?" Chambrun said.

"Bringing help," I said. "One Peter Williams who was once Neil Drury's best friend. He's down the hall in my apartment."

Wexler glanced down at a notebook that lay open in his lap. "Peter Williams, only survivor of the Drury disaster; blinded by the kidnappers. We know all about him, but it didn't seem much use asking for his help. He can't see. We need someone who can point Drury out to us."

"He'd know his voice anywhere, no matter how Drury disguised it. He might also be able to smell him," I said, perfectly straight-faced.

I saw Chambrun's eyes widen, and there was pleasure in them. "Something you overlooked, Mr. Wexler," he said. " 'Smell him'! Well, well!"

"Blind men sometimes have extraordinary extrasensory gifts," Wexler said, entirely amiable. "I should have taken the time to talk to him. I'm grateful to you for bringing him here, Mr.—?"

"Haskell," I said. "Public relations for the hotel."

"I'm George Wexler, in charge of this caper," he said.

There was a growling sound from Chambrun. "A caper," he said, "in case you don't read mystery fiction, Mark, is a slang word for 'case.'"

Wexler chuckled. "Sorry, Mr. Chambrun. I didn't know you were a purist." He put his pipe in his pocket, took out another one, and began to fill it from an oilskin pouch. "Your Peter Williams, Haskell, and the girl are our best hope of identifying Drury. Let us pray."

"What girl?" I asked.

He looked down at his notebook again. "Laura Malone. A hooker. Drury lived with her for about a year before the tragedy."

"A 'hooker,'" Chambrun said to me, with mock patience, "is a high-class call girl or prostitute."

Jerry Dodd turned from the window for the first time. He is short, dark, with very bright blue eyes. A shrewd operator, Jerry, who was one of a few people in whom Chambrun placed complete trust. Miss Ruysdale was another, and I hoped I was.

"You mean a guy like Drury paid for his tail?" Jerry asked.

"I think they were in love," Wexler said. "They met in Hollywood. She moved in with him—for about a year. The last time she saw him was the night he got word about his family. She thinks she would know him, no matter how changed he is. One of our men is flying her in from the Coast. She should be here early evening."

"She go back into business for herself?" Jerry asked.

"I don't know for sure," Wexler said. "My man will have all the dope on her when he gets here. Now, Dodd, what I need from you is a course in how to keep our men from standing out like sore thumbs in the hotel's daily routine."

"It depends on who's looking whether a thumb looks sore

or not," Jerry said. "Your men can never hide themselves from the staff."

Wexler took out of his pocket a paper that was a copy of the floor plan Ruysdale had given me. "This is clear enough," he said, "but it covers only one corridor, one bank of elevators, one fire stair. I need a guided tour from roof to subcellar; I need to see every emergency exist, every linen closet, every conceivable hiding place."

"Every room in the hotel is a hiding place," Chambrun said. "Are you suggesting that we invade six hundred rooms?"

"I want to know how to invade them if I need to," Wexler said.

Jerry Dodd grinned at him. "The kind of tour you want could take a couple of days, Mr. Wexler. The Beaumont is like a small city within itself."

Wexler glanced at his watch. "We have about twenty-two hours," he said. He stood up. "I have an appointment with the FBI."

"When do you want to start taking your tour?" Jerry asked.

Wexler smiled. "I'll have a man ready for you in ten minutes."

"Is there anything I can do for you, Mr. Wexler?" Chambrun asked. You could cut the acid in the air.

Wexler held a lighter to his pipe, looking at Chambrun through the little clouds of blue smoke. "I know you resent my intrusion here, Mr. Chambrun. I would if I were in your shoes. I'm sorry. I need your help to keep the boat from rocking while we try to prevent a murder that could turn the world upside-down. I need your special knowledge of the locale and the routines." He smiled. "I promise you, if it will make you feel any better, you can have a free kick at my behind when it's all over."

Chambrun's heavy lids lifted. "I stand properly rebuked for being childish," he said. "Count on us."

"Good man," Wexler said. He walked to the door and turned back. He spoke to me. "I'll want to talk to your Mr. Williams," he said. "Perhaps it would save time if we waited until Laura Malone gets here and we can pool their information about Drury."

"You name the time," I said.

I watched him leave. Not a bad guy, I thought. I don't think he underestimated Chambrun. But if I stood to have my head served up for lunch in the White House if I failed, I guess I'd want to play it my way.

Chambrun walked over to the sideboard and his beloved Turkish coffee maker. I think he was a little embarrassed by the way he had treated Wexler.

"I congratulate you on finding Williams, Mark," he said. "I think we should not wait for Drury's girl friend to start pumping him for every detail he can give us about Drury. I suggest you make Williams your number one priority."

"To be really useful to us he needs a chance to orient himself in the hotel," I said. "I already have a good deal about Drury from his former agent, as well as some from Peter."

"Your job," Chambrun said. "Hop to it."

I walked down the hall to my apartment and opened the door with my key. Just inside the door I froze. Peter Williams was sitting in the leather armchair that faced the door. Standing over him was a man, a huge man, built like a defensive tackle on a pro football team. He turned to look at me and I saw that he was Chinese; high cheekbones, straight, slightly flattened nose, and a wide, smiling mouth. His black eyes were only a little slanted, bright and hostile. His powerful body seemed to be straining against the very well tailored jacket of a tropical worsted suit.

"Mark?" Peter asked, the black glasses turn my way.

"Yes, Peter."

"As you can see, we have a visitor. He is Mr. Li Sung, General Chang's chief of staff, it seems."

Mr. Sung smiled at me, and then said, in surprisingly colloquial English: "Hi, man."

CHAPTER 4

I closed the door and stood with my back to it. "How did he get in?" I asked.

"I let him in," Peter said, "proud that I could walk to the door without bumping into anything."

"So, keep your shirt on, buster," Mr. Sung said. His smile widened. I saw that his lips weren't smiling. "You're wondering how come I'm not talking to you with Charlie Chan gobbledeguck. University of Southern Cal, class of sixty-three."

"Football?" I asked.

"Shot-put and hammer throw," Mr. Sung said. His smile faded. "Shall we get down to brass tacks, Mr. Haskell?"

"What kind of brass tacks?" I asked.

"Mr. Sung wants me to leave the hotel," Peter said.

"Correction," Mr. Sung said. "I don't just want Peter-baby to leave the hotel; I order it."

I saw then that one of the reasons his jacket seemed so tight was that Mr. Sung was wearing a shoulder holster.

"An order has to be backed up by the authority to issue

it," I said.

"Oh, boy, man, let's not get technical," Mr. Sung said. "My job is to guarantee the safety of General Chang. General Chang has enemies. One of them is a man named Neil Drury who has promised to kill him. Now, Mark-baby, you produce Peter-baby. Peter-baby has been Neil Drury's very close friend ever since they were kids in knee pants. So it is clear that Peter-baby will do anything he can to help his friend. So he is dangerous to me and to my General Chang. So I order him to leave the hotel." He shrugged. "So if it'll make you feel better, Mark-baby, I 'advise' him to leave the hotel. Because if he blinks his eyes more than once I will shoot a very large hole in his belly." He patted the holster bulge near his left armpit. He was making no bones about the gun. I guessed he probably had a permit signed in person by J. Edgar Hoover. Diplomatic privilege.

"George Wexler thanked me for bringing Peter here," I said. "He's in charge of protecting your general."

"Officially, baby," Mr. Sung said. "I will really protect him. So I advise Peter-baby to 'get out of town,' as the old song says. Because I will only have to get uneasy to give him the number-one treatment." He walked straight past me to the door, where he turned back. "You should know, Mark-baby, that I also know that Wexler is importing a lady friend of Neil Drury's. I have expressed disapproval but Wexler has ignored it. If you meet the lady you can tell her that I also advise her to get out of town. I do not choose to be surrounded by Neil Drury's friends."

"Would you believe that my only purpose in being here is to persuade Neil to give up his crusade?" Peter asked.

Mr. Sung grinned. "You can tell it to the marines," he said. He seemed proud of his outdated slang. He opened the door and went out.

Peter leaned his head back against the chair. "A comic-strip heavy," he said.

"I'm not laughing," I said. "In spite of his custom-tailored suit and his attempt at sounding 'mod,' he strikes me as a very primitive man who won't bother to play by the rules."

"I can believe it," Peter said. His mouth tightened. "You may recall I've met General Chang and his gang before." He lifted a hand to touch the rim of his black goggles. "What woman was he talking about, do you know?"

"A girl named Laura Malone," I said, still thinking about Mr. Sung.

Peter sat up very straight in his chair. "Laura Malone?"

"According to Wexler she's a 'hooker' who shacked up with Drury for a while."

Peter laughed, a mirthless laugh. "Oh, my God," he said.

"You know about her?" I asked.

He relaxed back against the chair again. "Yes, I know about her. Why is she coming here?"

"Apparently the supersleuths have been checking out on Drury's past to find friends or associates who might help them identify him when and if he shows. The girl thinks she would know him no matter how changed his face may be." I laughed. "They overlooked you because they knew you couldn't see him."

"She might know him at that," Peter said. It was almost as if he was thinking out loud. "They were very close to getting married when Neil's world caved in."

"Married?" I said. I guess the surprise sounded in my voice. "I mean—if she's what Wexler said—?"

Peter smiled. "You sound like a New England church deacon, Mark. You can sell out your business partner, your community, your church, your state, and if you repent you are accepted back into your world. But if you're a woman and you sell your body, no amount of repentance will do you any good. You're in the scarlet letter department forever." He moistened his lips. "Neil told me about her on a trip he made East a month before his world blew up. He fully intended to marry her and he wanted me to understand because he knew I'd hear the talk that was bound to circulate."

"Wexler said they lived together for a year."

"They had," Peter said. "Neil met her at a party somewhere. He was footloose, a bachelor, not involved at the moment. She was an extraordinarily beautiful, sexy girl. It was a routine, sort of 'night out' thing for him. He invited her to leave the party and they went to some sort of nightspot for a drink or two. Then he invited her to his house, to listen to some records or see his etchings or what-have-you. It was perfectly clear what he wanted and she seemed quite willing. A lovely evening,—he thought. When they got to his house something happened, something in the conversation. She thought he knew what she was—a professional. Something he said made it clear he didn't. He wasn't shocked, only amused that he'd been had. He made some wisecrack about perhaps a professional could teach him something. It was all quite impersonal now. No longer a conquest. He took her to bed, expecting nothing but technique. Somewhere along the way he realized it was more than that. There was a kind of special electricity about it. He found himself wishing he hadn't gone through with it—because he felt something for her.

"Sometime toward morning, when he was half asleep, she got up and dressed. He came to, seeing her standing beside the bed, ready to go. He asked her how much he owed her. She told him, quite without any emotion, that it was 'on the house.' Before he could pull his wits together she was gone."

"The prostitute with the heart of gold," I said.

The corner of Peter's mouth twitched. "That's what Neil thought. An odd experience; an unusually satisfying, impersonal piece. But he couldn't get her out of his mind. He wanted to see her again. He hadn't bothered to get her address or phone number. At the time, having found out about her, he'd assumed it was simply a one-night stand. He went back to his friend at whose party he'd met her, took a lot of kidding, and found out how to reach her. He called her and invited her to dinner. She turned him down. He called her again and she hung up on him. He went to where she lived and presented himself at her door. Reluctantly, she let him in. She looked, he told me, as though she'd been crying. She told him, in a kind of dead monotone, that she couldn't afford to involve herself except professionally. She couldn't afford, she told him, to get to like someone. They would hate her in the end for what she was, and she simply wouldn't allow herself to be hurt. The going was tough enough without that.

"He suggested she take a vacation from her work and come to live with him. It was crazy, he told me, but he wanted her more than he had ever wanted a woman in his life. They spent that whole evening together, going from nightspot to nightspot, arguing the point. Along toward morning she went home with him—and never left him again. It was, he told me, the most perfect relationship he'd ever had. Not just the sex part of it. It was a genuine love, filled with compassion and understanding. She anticipated his needs, understood his moods. It was, he told me, an overwhelming pleasure just to be in the room with her. She was a woman, he said, instinctively dedicated to just one thing— to be everything to her man. *disgusting slavery*

"He talked of marriage to her early. He wanted to give

34

her everything he had to give. This she wouldn't buy at first. She had to be sure the past wouldn't floor him when he was reminded of it, and he would be reminded of it by some 'kind people' if he married her. People, she knew, were laughing at him now behind his back because he was living with a call girl. She didn't have to have a title, she told him. But at the end of about eleven months of persistence from him she finally agreed.

"That was when he came to New York and told me about it. He wanted me, his best friend, to know the truth about it, no matter what people said, what the gossip was." Peter drew a deep breath. "Actually it was just two days after that I took off for South America in my job for Neil's father. And a month later—" His hand moved vaguely toward the black goggles. "Yes," he said, "I think she might know him no matter how changed he is. She and he were two parts of one whole."

"He didn't go back to her—after South America?"

Peter shook his head. "When he got to South America he came to see me in the hospital. I was sick with horror and self-pity. He was a madman, seething for revenge. But he thought of her. He begged me, when I got back to America, to get in touch with her, to help her in any way I could. He was making financial arrangements for her.

" 'But surely you'll see her,' I said."

"He shook his head. 'Not till I have squared accounts with this Chinese butcher,' he said. 'And I don't expect to come out of that alive. If I see her I might be persuaded to forget what's happened to my family.'

"I should have told him then that was exactly what he should do. That he couldn't win. But just then I was as eager as he was for revenge."

"Did you ever get in touch with Laura Malone?"

"When I got back to New York, and was able to forget my own problems for ten minutes, I put through a telephone call to her. She was no longer in Neil's house. It had been rented to some actor out there to make a film. They had no idea where Laura Malone was. It took nearly a month for acquaintances of mine to find her. She was working as a receptionist in some film company offices. She talked to me on the phone, polite, remote. She didn't need any help, thank you. No, she hadn't seen Neil. She didn't expect to. There had been a letter ending things. That was that."

"But she's evidently ready to help now," I said.

The black goggles were focused on the far wall. "She loves him," he said.

It was about six-thirty in the afternoon when I reported back to Chambrun in his office. The girls in Atterbury's office and mine had completed their checkout routine on the hotel guests. The results were even better than Chambrun had forecast. There were just four men registered in the Beaumont who didn't check out satisfactorily on the first go-round.

Chambrun had the cards on his desk when I got there and was discussing them with Jerry Dodd. I interrupted to tell them about our visit from Mr. Li Sung. His face had a rock-hard look to it that I knew very well.

"I have tried, through personal contacts, to get the State Department to make some sense for us," he said. "No luck. I have pointed out to them that Chang's men could promote a blood bath here at the Beaumont, or anywhere else they may stay. I've tried to convince them that Chang should be protected by our people alone, not his. No dice. They have pointed out that if a high official of this country— the President for example—travels abroad he is surrounded by our own secret service people as well as the local security people. That's true, of course, except that we know they won't mow down anyone whose looks they don't like. I'm told I must assume the same thing about Chang's men."

"Change is a butcher," Jerry said.

"He has said he was never in South America," I said.

Chambrun made an impatient gesture. "We live in a constantly changing diplomatic climate," he said. "Five years ago Chang was a barbarian Communist enemy. Today he is an accepted member of the world community. His past crimes are wiped off the slate." Chambrun lit one of his Egyptian cigarettes. "I've lived through this before—back in the dark days."

He referred to the "dark days" from time to time. That was when he had fought in the French underground in the last years of World War II.

"Just across the border from us was Franco, the Spanish dictator, friend of Hitler and Mussolini. We have tried, convicted, jailed, and executed German war criminals. But Franco, their friend and collaborator, is now treated with respect and courtesy. That is what is known as diplomatic expediency." He brought the palm of his hand down hard on the desk. "So that's the game we have to play—smile and bow and offer all our courtesies to a cold-blooded murderer and torturer. Diplomatic expediency!"

"Should I get Peter away from here?" I asked. "Sung made it clear he was a ready target; also the Malone girl when she gets here."

"It's up to them," Chambrun said. "They may be able to help us spot Drury and turn him off. We need them, but I wouldn't ask them to stay if they feel it's asking too much."

"I think Peter wants to stay," I said. "If something happens to Drury, it's a victory for Chang, and he has his own thoughts about Chang, poor bastard."

"Chang knows he has those thoughts," Chambrun said. "He may think Peter Williams is just as dangerous as Drury. I would if I were in his shoes."

"You think he's offered to help to cover his own desire to be on the scene—maybe take his own flier at Chang?" Jerry asked.

"He can't do anything without help," I said.

"And Drury would help if he's here, and probably the girl, and maybe dozens of other people right under our roof whom we have no way of guessing about."

"I really think he's deeply fond of Drury," I said, "and that his one concern is to help keep him from being uselessly wiped out."

Chambrun's eyes narrowed. "It will make it easier for you to share your rooms with him if you keep on believing that, Mark," he said. He reached for the four cards on his desk. "Robert Zabielski, a salesman from Cleveland, Ohio."

"About thirty," Jerry Dodd said. "Address a phony. Been here two days, so he hasn't paid a bill. We haven't seen a personal check or a traveler's check. Made his reservation ten days ago, the same day Chang's visit was announced in the press. He's about five feet eight inches tall, overweight. Wouldn't seem to fit Drury's specifications."

"Habits?"

"He drinks in the Trapeze about this time of day. A gal has joined him there the first two nights. She doesn't live in the hotel but she's gone to his room with him both nights. Room service records indicate they do some solid drinking without any eating."

"What do they drink?"

"Sour-mash bourbon—by the bottle!"

"No vodka?"

"No vodka."

"Next," Chambrun said. "Paul Wells."

"Old man, I'd guess in his early seventies," Jerry said. "He gave a Philadelphia address. It checks—but he's only lived there about six weeks. A sort of rooming house. Cheap place. One wouldn't think he could afford our prices. Been here three days. Spends most of his time in the hotel—the Trapeze, the Blue Lagoon Room, the Spartan Bar. He pays cash for everything. His bill will have nothing but his room on it. He's about six feet tall, thin. Right specifications, wrong age."

"Drury is an actor. He could age himself," Chambrun said.

"Bald as an egg," Jerry said.

"Next is Sam Schwartz," Chambrun said.

"Hollywood address. Hotel—the Spencer Arms. Flea bag. Lived there for about a year. Talks a great ball game to the hotel people out there about his big film deals. Carries a roll that would choke a horse, lavish spender. But a quick check of the people we know in the film business indicates no one has ever heard of him."

"But he checks out in a way," Chambrun said.

"He's had that hotel room for a year, but according to them he's away most of the time—weeks on end. Where he goes, nobody knows. He's the right height, right weight, has an ugly scar on his right cheek that could be a phony, or the result of clumsy surgery. Doesn't drink. Leaves the hotel here in the morning and doesn't come back until late evening. Been here a week. No phone calls. He has his room for four more days."

"And finally James Gregory," Chambrun said.

"Came in three days ago," Jerry said. "Gave his address as a private clinic on Long Island. Suffers from emphysema. Hasn't been out of his room since he got here. No phone calls. He has seen Doc Partridge, who says he's in bad shape. Lives with an oxygen tank by his side. Seems to just lie in his bed and read papers and magazines. He reserved his room for two weeks. The clinic on Long Island vouches for him; long-time patient. There's something odd about it, though."

"Odd?"

"This clinic specializes in cosmetic surgery. Most of the patients are women getting their noses bobbed, their ears trimmed, or their faces lifted. The head man is a Dr. Coughlin, who has a big and good reputation in the field. I got Doc Partridge to call him."

Dr. Partridge is the Beaumont's house physician.

"And?" Chambrun asked.

"Doc pretended he needed to know something about the case."

"Why did Gregory call in Doc?" Chambrun asked.

"He has to take injections of some sort—Gregory does. He can't give them to himself. All perfectly normal for his kind of sickness, Doc says. Coughlin was apparently perfectly open with Doc. Gregory is an old friend, Coughlin says. A writer who's spent his life traveling around the world. Now he's trapped by his sickness—his oxygen needs. Coughlin took him into the clinic so that he could look out for him personally. Gregory wanted a change and Coughlin, who has a blue card in our file, made the reservation for him."

A blue card is a top credit and past performance top-drawer record at the Beaumont.

"But you have his friend on your list," Chambrun said.

"Just the coincidence of his connection with a cosmetic surgeon," Jerry said. "Coughlin just could be the man who took care of Drury. Our man with the oxygen tank could be scouting out the lay of the land for Drury."

"But you say he doesn't leave his room," I said.

Jerry nodded. "General Chang isn't here yet," he said.

It was then that Chambrun and Jerry and I went up to the twelfth floor to look at the arrangements Atterbury had made to receive Chang, his staff and bodyguards, and the FBI and CIA boys. Wexler joined us there, pipe suspended from one corner of his mouth. His tweed suit looked as if he'd slept in it. The little crow's-foot lines at the corners of his eyes looked deeper than they had earlier.

Mr. Atterbury, who is highly efficient but a little fruity, was to be our guide. He was perspiring and somewhat flustered, it seemed.

"There are two rooms at the far end of the corridor that won't be vacated for another hour," he said.

"We have till tomorrow afternoon," Wexler said, cheerfully.

Atterbury, as if he was conducting a museum tour, started to describe the layout, but Wexler checked him. "It's the same as the floor plan I saw earlier?" he asked.

"Yes, sir."

The reserved rooms were on both sides of a dead-end hallway. The rooms on the east side of the hall had a view of the river. From the windows there was a sheer drop of twelve stories to the street below. The rooms on the west side opened onto an eleven-story drop to the glass roof covering the main lobby. The gap to the opposite wing was a good fifty yards. There was no way to breach it, unless you could fly. The closed end of what was in effect a three-sided rectangle was occupied by a bank of elevators.

Wexler had already filled in his floor plan. At the mouth of the corridor were rooms for the FBI men and the CIA. Chang's people lined each side of the hall until you came to the suite that was on the east side of the hall. First, south of the suite was a double room for two of the personal bodyguards. Another double, directly across from the suite, was to be occupied by the other two personal bodyguards. The final single room on the east side was to be for Chang's lady secretary, and opposite that the room for his valet. If you wanted to rush the suite, it would be like the charge of the Light Brigade—cannons to the left of you, cannons to the right of you.

Wexler expressed himself as pleased. "The only other thing, Mr. Atterbury, is some comfortable chairs to be placed at the mouth of the corridor. There will always be armed sentinels stationed outside the rooms."

Chambrun spoke for the first time. "When did Li Sung check into the hotel, Atterbury?"

Atterbury has a photographic memory. He dreams of registration forms. I daresay he could give you the name and room number of every guest in the hotel without referring to notes.

"There is no one by that name registered in the hotel, Mr. Chambrun," he said, "unless he has checked in, in the last ten minutes, and there has been no reservation made for a person of that name."

Wexler cocked an eyebrow at Chambrun. "He's Chang's top man," he said. "Not due till tomorrow."

"He was here a little while ago," Chambrun said. He nodded to me and I told Wexler about Sung's cheery visit with Peter and me.

"Describe him," Wexler said, scowling.

I did my best. Sung's size had been the most memorable thing about him. His size and his speech.

Wexler chuckled. "That's Li-baby," he said.

"You had some reason to doubt it?" Chambrun asked.

Wexler rubbed the bowl of his pipe against the side of his nose. "Neil Drury isn't our only problem," he said. "General Chang has a rather extraordinary assortment of enemies: dissidents in his own country, the Chinese on Formosa, people from other Asian countries who are hard to distinguish from Chinese, due to the color of their skins, unless you

42

are an expert. Oh, we have a list of a couple of dozen people in addition to Drury that we'll be watching for."

Chambrun's forehead was split by a deep frown. "A shooting gallery, that's what you're setting up for us, Mr. Wexler."

"But can you think of anyone better equipped to help us deal with the problem than you and your staff, Mr. Chambrun?"

Chambrun grunted. "Flattery will get you no place," he said.

Peter Williams was listening to the seven o'clock news on radio when I rejoined him in my rooms. I suggested a drink.

"If it wouldn't be too boring for you, Mark, I'd like very much to have a drink in one of the public places—the Trapeze Bar, for example. I've got to begin to learn to find my way around. There's so little time."

"Why not?" I said.

I telephoned down to Mr. Del Greco, the captain in the Trapeze, and asked him to set aside a table for us. Six o'clock is about the busiest time down there, with people stopping off for cocktails before dinner.

The Trapeze Bar is almost literally suspended in space over the foyer to the Grand Ballroom below it. The walls are a kind of iron grillwork, and some artist of the Calder school has designed a collection of mobiles of circus performers operating on trapezes. The faint circulation of air from a conditioner keeps these little figures constantly in motion. The patrons of the Trapeze at this time of day are apt to be rather elegantly dressed. It isn't a saloon where you just step in off the street for a slug. It is a gathering place for social celebrities, political figures, famous stage and film personalities. It's popular with this sort of customer because there are no kids hanging around with autograph books, almost never any of the gawking curious. The important and the famous and infamous can enjoy themselves there without the danger of outside interference. Mr. Del Greco, who looks like a Spanish grandee, runs a very tight ship.

As Peter and I went down in the elevator to the lobby and then up the short flight of stairs to the Trapeze, I wondered how he prepared himself. Did he count the steps? Did special smells, noises, other details register permanently with him—things I wouldn't think about or be aware of because I can see?

Mr. Del Greco greeted us with his usual courtesy and took us to a corner table. Several people nodded to me as we took our place. I must have known three-quarters of the people in the room as regular customers. I introduced Peter to Del Greco and made sure he'd be properly cared for if he came there alone.

As we waited for our drinks—a Jack Daniels on the rocks for me and coffee for Peter—I caught him up on things. I was particularly interested to know if any of our four question-mark guests rang any sort of bell with him, or Dr. Coughlin, the face-changing surgeon.

"Never heard of any of them," he said. He sipped his coffee, which the waiter had brought. "I told you before, I have no idea where Neil got his face changed." He smiled faintly. "I'm curious to know how you know he has had it changed."

"That's what the CIA tells us. It seems to be accepted as a fact."

"Neil was an expert at makeup," Peter said. "He'd easily change his appearance almost totally. I've been wondering if perhaps he circulated the rumor on purpose. He could then appear with a half dozen different faces while you're looking for one new one."

44

"Oh, brother!" I said.

"With all the cops and bodyguards surrounding him, how is the hotel involved in protecting Chang?" he asked.

"Details connected with service," I said. "Mr. Fresney, the head chef, will supervise every ounce of food that goes to Chang's party. Food could be tampered with."

"Poison?"

"A possibility," I said. "Jerry Dodd, our security chief, will have men on the twelfth floor checking out on every bellboy, waiter, maid, housekeeper who appears there. No outsider dressed like a waiter is going to get into Chang's area. We know our people. Without us the professionals would have to check everyone each time they appeared. From the front doorman to the linen maid we'll be constantly watching The people on our telephone switchboard will be monitoring incoming calls—listening for cranks and crackpots and trying to trace any such calls that may come in. Our people will double what is the usual patrolling of the hotel, all the fire stairs, back corridors which aren't used by the public, the basement areas, the roof. It would take Wexler's people a month to learn what to look for."

Peter swirled the coffee in his cup. "What about bombs, which are the pet playthings of today's assassins?"

"Tomorrow morning every inch of every room reserved for Chang's party will be searched, and after that sealed off. From that moment on the whole twelfth floor will be under constant surveillance by our people. Wherever Chang goes in the hotel our people will be present outside the perimeter of his own bodyguards. We hope he will let us know when and where he proposes to go, but if he doesn't, we'll still be with him."

"Sounds pretty tight. Can you trust your own people?"

"The ones assigned to this job, yes. I'd bet my life on each of them. No one will perform any service for General Chang who isn't known to us for a long time, completely trustworthy."

I signaled the waiter for a second round of drinks.

Peter leaned back in his chair. "I'll bet you're looking around as you talk for a five-foot-eleven-inch man, weighing about a hundred and sixty-five pounds, whom you don't know," he said.

"I guess that'll stay true till this is over," I said. "What about you?"

He cocked his head slightly to one side. "I can hear things that you can't hear," he said. "Conversations that are just a mumbling sound to you are rather embarrassingly clear to me. There is a couple sitting about fifteen feet away from us, to my left. Can you describe them to me?"

I knew the couple he was talking about. The man, a florid, white-haired guy in his sixties, was the president of a big machine-tool manufacturing company from the Mid-west. He came to the Beaumont about four times a year and he spent money like water. The letter *W* was marked on his card—woman chaser. The girl with him was a very expensive call girl. Oh, we see call girls in the hotel. You may ask why we allow it. These girls, called "hookers" by Wexler, are a part of our world. As long as they don't get potted and don't make public scenes there isn't much we can do about it.

I told Peter who they were, what they looked like. The girl was a very lush redhead.

Peter smiled. "Would it surprise you to know that the gentleman is urging her to come upstairs with him before dinner, where they will take off their clothes and she will delight him by whipping him?"

"Good God!"

"I'm not always sure that I enjoy this acute hearing," Peter

46

said. Even as he spoke my industrialist put a twenty-dollar bill down on the table and he and the girl walked out together.

"He won the day," I said. "They're leaving."

Peter shrugged. "He's paying for it. Why not?"

At the doorway our couple was almost knocked down by Jerry Dodd. He stood there, looking around, spotted us, and came toward us, almost running. I knew him well enough to be certain something out of the ordinary had happened. He reached us, stood by my chair breathing hard.

"Li Sung," he said.

"What about him?"

"He went out a window from somewhere high up," he said. "Very dead."

I heard Peter's breath exhale in a quavering sound. He was gripping the edge of the table with both hands.

"He's here," he said. "Neil is here!"

Part Two

CHAPTER 1

There was no sign of any excitement in the Trapeze or in the main lobby of the hotel. Li Sung had spattered himself on the pavement on the north side street. Most people came into the hotel through the Fifth Avenue entrance. I saw that Mike Maggio, the night bell captain, was standing by the revolving door on the side street. He had evidently locked it shut so that hotel patrons, unaware of violence, wouldn't walk out into the center of police, photographers, and the smashed body of Li Sung, covered by a canvas tarpaulin.

Sudden death is not a rarity in a big city hotel. There are always those elderly gentlemen who have heart attacks in the wrong rooms; the Beaumont, most expensive of all the city's hostelries, quite naturally had a large clientele of older people, and older people die unexpectedly; and suicides are not uncommon. Lonely and desperate people are apt to go to a hotel, away from friends and family, when they are contemplating self-destruction. They stay alone, locked in their rooms, trying to decide what to do with themselves. Then there is the bathtub with its hot water and a razor blade, or the sleeping pills, or the open window, or, not infrequently, the belt or the bathrobe cord and the heels kicking together above the level of the floor.

The one or two people who were stopped at the side door by Mike Maggio were told that someone had jumped. Neither Jerry nor Peter nor I considered for a moment the possibility of suicide. Jerry is an old hand at spotting dangerously depressed people. Mr. Atterbury and Karl Nevers, the chief desk clerk, and Johnny Thacker and Mike Maggio have a nose for it. I know of at least a dozen would-be suicides who have been stopped because these trained people knew the signs and acted accordingly. Li Sung, arrogant, in a position of power, riding the crest of Chang's diplomatic position, would never in God's world have jumped willingly out a top-story window

One of Jerry's men stopped him as we were approaching the elevators.

"We still don't know where he took the dive from, Jerry," the man said.

"Keep looking."

"Right. They'll need a vacuum cleaner to pick him up. He's spread around the sidewalk like a smashed pumpkin. One item. He was armed, but the gun is still snug in its holster."

"I'm on my way to the boss's office," Jerry said. "Call me there if there's anything new. Cops on the job yet?"

"Dozens of 'em. I called Lieutenant Hardy, like you said, in case it should be a homicide."

"There's no 'in case' about it, Mac," Jerry said.

Miss Ruysdale, looking cool and efficient, waved us into Chambrun's office. She should have been home long ago, but there she was. That is the extraordinary thing about her. She is always there when she is needed. I wondered what had kept her late tonight.

Wexler was with the boss, and a man introduced to us as Agent Larch of the FBI, a sleek, dark, quiet man.

"I found them in the Trapeze," Jerry said, gesturing toward Peter and me. I introduced Peter.

There were polite hellos.

"No question that it's Li Sung?" Wexler asked.

"None," Jerry said. "There was a wallet in his coat pocket, diplomatic passport, the works. He was carrying a gun."

"He had a gun when he visited us," I said. "Shoulder holster, like I told you."

"You know yet where he came from?" Larch asked.

"Not yet," Jerry said. "There are over five hundred windows on that side of the house. We're starting from the top, the way he smashed up. A few stories up wouldn't have spread him around the way he is. Most of the rooms are occupied. Takes time. You have to explain to people before you can get in."

"Fire escapes?"

"Only at the very low levels," Jerry said. "Up above you use the inside fire stairs in an emergency."

"It couldn't have been easy to force him out a window," Larch said. "He was a big man, an athlete, a trained fighter, karate expert. I wouldn't have wanted to tackle him myself."

"The gun is still in its holster," Jerry said. "He evidently didn't get to draw it."

"We'll have to wait for the medical examiner to know whether the fall killed him—or something else," Larch said. "I don't think anyone could have forced him out a window while he was alive—or conscious. You'll find a bullet in him, or some other kind of wound."

"If you can put him together to find it," Jerry said.

Wexler looked very tired. "There's going to be hell to pay," he said. He turned his somber eyes toward Peter, who was standing, rigid, beside me. "You can imagine the first thought I have, Mr. Williams. From the information we have, Li Sung was one of General Chang's men in South America five years ago."

"He may have been," Peter said, in a faraway voice.

"Would Neil Drury know that?"

"He'd know that anyone connected with Chang, then or now, was his enemy," Peter said.

Larch lit a cigarette and let the smoke out in a long sigh. "Look here, Mr. Williams," he said, "you'll have to understand that I can only guess what your own feelings are. I have to assume that Li Sung's death isn't a heartbreak for you."

"Hardly."

"Nor would you go into mourning if anything happened to General Chang."

"No."

"Yet you came here to help us prevent it."

"Not exactly," Peter said. "I came here to try to help keep Neil Drury from walking into an almost certain death-trap set up by Chang."

"I don't follow," Larch said.

"It's quite simple," Chambrun said, speaking for the first time, with some impatience. "Mr. Williams thinks Chang would plan to let Drury get through to him, and then mow him down."

"Is that it, Mr. Williams?"

"That's it," Peter said. "You want the truth? If I thought Neil had a chance of succeeding I'd be home, minding my own business."

"The first thing Williams said when I told him what had happened was, 'He's here. Neil is here,'" Jerry said.

"You have any way to know that for certain, Mr. Williams," Wexler asked.

"It was my first thought," Peter said. "I can't know it for

certain. There are plenty of poor bastards around the world who'd like to see Chang—or Li Sung—dead. Neil's only one of a small army. One very dedicated member of that army."

"You haven't heard from him recently?"

"Not since about a month after South America. Almost five years."

"If he did this would you help him to get away if you could?" Larch asked.

"I would."

"It's hard to figure out just whose side you're on, Mr. Williams," Larch said.

"Not at all. I'm on Neil's side." Peter's voice shook slightly. "I would help get him to Chang if I knew how; I'd help him to escape if I could. I came here to stop him from trying the impossible. I don't want him to lose his life failing."

"Maybe he didn't fail this afternoon."

"If it was Neil, he succeeded because no one was protecting Li Sung and Li Sung didn't think of himself as a target, so he was careless. Chang will have his own Chinese wall around him, as well as you people. Another story."

Wexler shook his head. "I'm not sure we can risk accepting your help, Mr. Williams."

"That's up to you," Peter said.

The door behind us opened and I turned around to see Miss Ruysdale standing there. "Mr. Wexler, there is a man of yours here, a Mr. Craven. He has a young woman with him, a Miss Malone."

"Please ask them to come in," Wexler said.

That was when I first saw Laura Malone.

I set that sentence apart because it was a moment in my life I'm not going to forget. Not ever.

I can't describe her, because I don't have words that will convey exactly what she was like. She was not tall, five feet four or five. She was wearing a dark dress, skirt just down to the middle of her kneecaps. She was carrying a tan cloth coat over her arm. Her hair was blonde, a golden blonde, worn shoulder length. Her eyes were wide, a kind of a lapis blue—dark blue, with the suggestion of banked fires. Her mouth was wide and generous, and I thought her lips trembled slightly as she faced us. Her figure was perfect— not overlush but perfect. Pass her on the street and you'd have thought she was an unusually pretty girl, but nothing sensational. Find yourself looking into those extraordinary eyes and you were hooked. She seemed to aim her total attention on Peter, who hadn't turned her way.

There was the babble of Wexler's hurried introductions. I don't know what he said because I couldn't take my eyes off Laura. She came toward me, went past me, and put her hand on Peter's arm.

"You are Neil's Peter Williams?" she asked. Her voice was low, husky. I found it enchanting.

"Yes," Peter said, not reacting.

"We talked once, long ago," she said.

"Yes."

"I'm glad you're here," she said. "Someone to talk to." Then, when he didn't answer. "Are you angry with me for coming here to help them stop Neil?"

He turned his head toward her and the black goggles focused on her. "It's all we can do if we care for him," he said.

"I'm glad you feel that way," she said. She took her hand away from his arm and turned to Wexler. "How do we do what we have to do?"

"You think, Miss Malone, you'd know Drury no matter

how changed his face is?" Wexler asked.

"If he was in the same room with me I would know it," she said.

"How?"

"We were in love," she said simply. "I am still in love. I would know." She saw the doubt in Wexler's face. "I would know his hands if I saw them. I'd know the little characteristic gestures he makes. I'd know the way he holds his head, as if he was listening. Like Peter, I'd know his voice no matter how he disguised it. I'd know, that's all."

"We think he is, or will be, here in the hotel," Chambrun said. "He will have to study the procedures we've set up to protect General Chang. It seems to me you will have to begin an endless circulating in the public places in the hotel. He will have to eat and drink. He will have to watch and study. If you're right about yourself, you're bound to encounter him sooner or later."

"Please God!" she whispered.

"They think Neil may already have killed one of Chang's men," Peter said.

"I wonder," Chambrun said. "I wonder if he would risk that luxury."

"He would if Li Sung recognized him," Jerry said.

"If Li Sung could recognize him, then Miss Malone and Mr. Williams are a cinch to make it," Chambrun said. He turned to me. "I've arranged a room for Miss Malone."

"I've already been there. It's very nice, thank you," she said.

"Then I suggest, Mark, that you instruct Miss Malone and Mr. Williams where to begin circulating. We need to find Drury, and find him fast."

The door behind us opened once more and there was Miss Ruysdale again, ushering in Mr. Roy Worthington

Foster, the State Department man. He was pale with anger.

"How could you have let this happen, Wexler?" he asked. He paid no attention to anyone else.

"We had no way of knowing that Li Sung was in this part of the world until a short time ago. Nobody notified us he was coming in advance of the General. Mr. Haskell told us less than an hour ago that he and Mr. Williams had been visited by Li Sung. Larch and I were trying to locate Sung when we got the word that he'd gone out a window."

"The word has gotten to General Chang," Foster said.

"How? Who passed it on?" Wexler asked.

"God knows," Foster said. His shoulders sagged.

"It's not hard to guess at," Chambrun said. "There's probably been someone in the hotel for days, under cover, smelling out the lay of the land for the General."

"There are no Chinese registered in the hotel at the moment," Larch said.

Chambrun looked disgusted. "It wouldn't be a Chinese," he said. "It wouldn't be anyone obvious."

"Well, there is hell to pay," Foster said. "Chang has been on the phone to Washington. If we can't protect his people he will take on the job himself—and damn the torpedoes. He's not waiting till tomorrow. He's on a jet plane now, arriving in about an hour. Are his quarters ready for him?"

"They can be," Chambrun said.

"And the protective setup?" Foster turned to the CIA man.

"Can do," Wexler said.

"If he isn't satisfied with what you've arranged for him you're going to have to accommodate him," Foster said. "That's from the very top in Washington."

"We could, of course, just turn over the country to him," Chambrun said.

Wexler's smile was tired. " 'Ours not to reason why, Ours but to do and die.' "

"Well, try to die some other place," Chambrun said. He turned to Jerry. "You'll have to make your bomb search now, Jerry. Notify Atterbury. Notify Mrs. Kniffin, the housekeeper on twelve. An hour doesn't give us very much time."

Larch followed Jerry out of the office, muttering about organizing his own men. Wexler didn't move. He was fumbling with his pipe and pouch. "I'm sorry about this, Chambrun," he said. "Between you and me, it's as if your hotel was about to be taken over by gangsters. There's nothing I can do to prevent it."

"Over my dead body," Chambrun said. His glittering black eyes were buried deep in their pouches. He glanced at his wristwatch. "We haven't much time. If you'll excuse me, Wexler, I have my own arrangements to make."

"Don't try to fight the General, Chambrun," Wexler said. "You can't win."

"I have only one interest in this matter," Chambrun said. "The routines of my hotel are not to be disturbed; my guests are not to be disturbed. I suggest you tell the General that when he arrives. Let him try to disrupt our normal functioning and he may find out some of the facts of life about the techniques of resistance."

"Good luck," Wexler said. "But don't overplay your hand. Let me know the minute the twelfth floor is ready for occupancy. The General won't want to be kept waiting."

"If he has to wait, he will wait—till we are ready," Chambrun said.

Wexler went out, a trail of pipe smoke drifting behind him.

"You want us to start circulating?" I asked.

"Wait," Chambrun said. He pressed a button on his

desk and Miss Ruysdale appeared.

"You heard it all, Ruysdale?" Chambrun asked.

She nodded. I realized the intercom switch on his desk had been open the whole time.

"I want to be present during the bomb search," Chambrun said. "Please convey some orders for me."

Ruysdale's notebook and pad were at the ready.

"You will contact Mr. Fresney in the kitchen," Chambrun said. "There will be no service to the twelfth-floor rooms without me, or Jerry, or Mark—or someone personally designated by me—going along to the rooms. Going into the rooms with the orders. Understood?"

"Yes."

"You'll get in touch with Mrs. Kiley." Mrs. Kiley is the night supervisor on our telephone switchboards. "All calls in and out of the twelfth floor setup will be monitored. That order will be conveyed to Mrs. Veach, the day supervisor."

"The General isn't going to like you listening in," I said.

"The General won't know, if Mrs. Kiley does her job properly," Chambrun said. "I want a transcript of all calls sent to me as they are made—except of course, room service orders. I'll get the word from the kitchen on those."

"I don't suppose monitoring will do much good," Peter said, "if they speak in Chinese."

"My dear Mr. Williams, members of almost all the UN delegations live here. We have multilingual operators on our switchboards. Chinese is no problem, I promise you." Chambrun turned back to Miss Ruysdale. "I want you to talk to the chief engineer. I want the entire bank of elevators to the twelfth floor under constant control. If I want the power off there, I want it done in a matter of seconds."

"Right."

"Get hold of the master electrician. I want the bug in the

General's suite activated."

"You've bugged the General's room?" I asked.

"In the air-conditioning unit," Chambrun said. "Long-playing tape."

"Suppose he finds it?"

Chambrun gave me a fleeting smile. "We'll blame it on Wexler," he said. "Get going, Ruysdale."

Miss Ruysdale evaporated.

I had been watching Laura Malone. She had moved away to the far wall and was studying the blue Picasso. She seemed not to have been listening to Chambrun's exchange with Ruysdale. Chambrun went over to the Turkish coffee maker.

"Anyone join me?" he asked.

Laura Malone turned away from the painting. "I'd love to," she said.

Chambrun brought her a small demitasse cup and put it down on one of the end tables beside an armchair.

"You drink it as it comes," he said. "Sugar or cream spoils its flavor." He stood beside her as she sat down, balancing his own cup and saucer in the palm of his left hand. He watched her as she tasted. She looked up at him and smiled. She had won him. Most people struggle to hide their dislike of that potent brew.

"I don't think we have the right to ask you and Mr. Williams to undertake this hunt for Drury," he said, moving toward his desk.

"Why not?" Peter asked, in a flat voice.

"Wexler described it pretty accurately," Chambrun said, sitting down in his high-backed chair. "Like gangsters taking over. Li Sung knew you were here. He may have reported before he died. Chang won't bother to guess whether you told Sung the truth—that you were here to warn Drury off. He'll lump you as the enemy. Drury is known to be a potential assassin. You are his friends. Cross Chang's path and he won't stop to weigh possibilities. He has the excuse of Li Sung's murder—because that's almost certainly what it was, murder. In this strange world of diplomacy he has a right to defend himself. He won't wait to ask for help from Wexler, or Larch, or anyone else. So I think you are both in the gravest kind of danger. Chang may want to kill just to get even for Li Sung."

Laura lowered her demitasse cup. "But you still want to locate Neil?"

Chambrun nodded. "Because he is Chang's number one target."

"Then I don't have any choice," she said quietly. "I don't know about Peter."

"Neither do I have a choice," Peter said.

"Then I'd like to suggest a game-plan for this situation," Chambrun said. "When Chang arrives, you two stay out of his way. He's going to be an angry man when he gets here, angry and secretly frightened. That's when a killer is most dangerous. No point in showing yourselves and inviting an instant reaction from him. Understood?"

"Yes," Laura said.

Peter's black goggles were focused on the blue Picasso, which he couldn't see.

"I don't believe Drury will try anything tonight," Chambrun said. "He'll probably wait until he's had a chance to study the precautionary plans Wexler has set up. I'm convinced he won't just take a pot shot at the General. He has to face him, to make sure Chang has a few moments to know the meaning of fear, to know why he is dying. If I'm wrong, it will take a miracle to stop him. If I'm right, he'll take time to choose the perfect moment, and that gives us a chance."

"What are we waiting for?" Peter asked. "Laura and I should start circulating."

"Listen to me," Chambrun said. "I don't believe in magic. I'm not a romantic. Maybe you'll recognize his voice, Williams. Maybe you have some special personal radar system, Miss Malone, that'll tell you Drury's nearby. I, personally, count on something else.

Laura was watching him intently.

"I count on his caring enough for you—both of you, but particularly Miss Malone—to want to get you away from here."

"Why?"

"Does it occur to you that Chang might try to use you as a hostage for his safety? Chang's best bet, if he doesn't choose to let Drury get to him, is to get hold of one or both of you and let Drury know what will happen to you if he doesn't give himself up."

I felt the small hairs rising on the back of my neck. Drury knew, God help him, what Chang did to hostages. We were crazy to use these two people, I told myself. They could be a way for Chang to help himself.

"Drury has made a study of Chang," Chambrun said. "He'll see that possibility at once. He'll be desperate to get you to give up, go away. So, I don't think you'll have to recognize his voice or feel some romantic stirrings. Give him the chance to get to you without attracting attention to himself and he'll take it."

Laura's fingers were gripping her black patent-leather handbag so tightly they had turned a dead white.

"So you don't circulate together," Chambrun said. "Mr. Williams, I suggest you go down to the grill room and have dinner. Take time with it. Mark will arrange with the captain there to give you a conspicuous table. If Drury spots you he may approach you or get some kind of message to you. You can't move around as readily as Miss Malone. Stay put. Pray."

"Right," Peter said.

Chambrun's narrowed eyes turned to Laura. "I suggest you go to the Blue Lagoon for a drink. We discourage lone women there, but Mark will arrange with Mr. Cardoza, the maître d'. Have a drink, move on to the Trapeze. We'll have somebody watching you in case of trouble."

"What kind of trouble?" Laura asked.

"A woman alone, circulating from bar to bar in this or any other hotel, attracts a special kind of attention," Chambrun said. "From wolves. The chances are you'll be invited to dinner, invited upstairs to a room. We'll be watching you, but we won't be able to move in too fast. It could always be Drury acting a part. We'll need some sort of indication from you that you need help."

Her voice was low, bitter. "I had experience with that sort of thing in the old days," she said.

"So you'll know how to handle it," Chambrun said. "I have one last piece of advice."

"Yes?"

"Run," he said. "Get as far away from here as you can as fast as you can."

Peter stood up. "Will you arrange for a table for me in the grill, Mark?" he asked.

Chambrun let his breath out in a long sigh. "Good luck," he said. "I think Mark shouldn't go with you. It could scare Drury off. The same for you, Miss Malone."

"I understand."

"Stay here for a few minutes until Mr. Williams gets settled in the grill, then start your ploy. And good luck to you both."

CHAPTER 2

When I look back on the extraordinary triple manhunt
that started that evening at the Beaumont, I realize that
there was a stretch of time, starting right then in Chambrun's office, when I was less than a totally efficient soldier
in Chambrun's army. I call it a triple manhunt because that's
what it was. Wexler and Larch and Chambrun were hunting
for Drury to prevent a murder and save his life. Chang and
his strong-arm boys and his elaborate staff would be hunting for Drury to eliminate him as a danger to the General
forever. And there was Lieutenant Hardy, an old friend of
ours at the Beaumont, attached to the homicide squad of
the New York police, who hadn't at that moment appeared
on the scene but who would be hunting for Drury, or Mr.
X, as the possible murderer of Li Sung.

In telling the story there is no point in delaying the reve-
lation of certain facts that came later in that first, turbu-
lent evening. On the roof of the Beaumont there are four
penthouse apartments. They are serviced by the hotel staff
but they are co-ops, owned by the tenants. One of them be-
longs to Mr. Battles, the Beaumont's owner. He has never
set foot in it so far as I know. Chambrun has lived in it for
twenty years. The other three owners are inconsequential
to this story, had nothing to do with it, though I suspect
they suffered a good deal under questioning from the FBI,
the CIA, Jerry Dodd, and later Lieutenant Hardy. None of
them saw anything, heard anything. One was a wonderfully

weird old lady, a Mrs. Haven, who lived alone in a Collier-brothers' jumble of relics of a past life, with a small, obnoxious, black-and-white Japanese spaniel. The others were two elderly couples, each living in a kind of old world elegance, lonely, uncurious. They were all beyond suspicion in the murder of Li Sung. If any of them had seen or heard anything they would have said so. They were law abiding, quiet, uninterested in anything but what they ate, whether they were hot or cold, whether the sun was out or not.

But they had all been within yards of a violence, because Li Sung, either before or after he was killed, had been thrown off the roof not ten yards from the heat-withered little garden that was part of Mrs. Haven's domain. There was a scuffed-up area in which there was a sample of human blood, and conclusively, there was a little piece of cloth that had been torn from Li Sung's jacket. The struggle had been brief. Mrs. Haven, known to us in the hotel as the Madwoman of Chaillot, stated flatly that nothing could have happened where it obviously had happened. She hadn't been out of her apartment since early afternoon when she'd walked her dog. If anything had happened out on the roof, Toto, the spaniel, would have given her warning. Toto, she insisted, was a perfect watchdog. Most of us in the hotel knew that Toto was too fat and lazy to have barked at anyone for years.

That's where Li Sung had been attacked—ten yards from Mrs. Haven's rear windows. He had been thrown over the parapet. When they scooped his remains up off the sidewalk, there was so little of him left in one piece that the medical examiner's report was not too definitive. It did suggest that there was evidence that Sung had been stabbed with some kind of knife or sharp, pointed instrument, but the condition of his body made it impossible to be very exact about it.

So much for what I didn't know when I was left alone in Chambrun's office with Laura Malone while Peter left for the grill and Chambrun headed for an inspection of the twelfth floor. I have said that I wasn't a totally efficient soldier in Chambrun's army at that moment. Laura Malone was the reason.

I don't know if I can explain it. Nothing quite like it had ever happened to me before. I am thirty-six years old, reasonably sophisticated. The world I lived and worked in, Chambrun's world, had made me a little cynical about people. I'd seen hundreds of attractive exteriors that covered hidden cesspools. Beautiful women swarm the corridors and public rooms of the Beaumont. You learn to look at them with a completely impersonal eye. God knows what beds they were tossing around in, or what sexual aberrations they enjoyed—like whipping elderly machine-tool manufacturers. Nothing looks good eough to me really to want until I have listened to them talk, till I have sampled their humor, till I know something about their tastes and predilections.

Laura Malone had walked into Chambrun's office and I was gone. I knew what she had been. I knew about her association with Neil Drury, to whom the same sort of instant involvement had evidently happened; I knew that she still loved Drury and that, according to Peter, they were still two parts of one whole. There wasn't the slightest reason to imagine that she would look at me twice. If she'd have any interest in anyone, it would be Peter, who had been her man's closest friend.

When I was a small boy my mother took me to some sort of children's play. I don't remember much about it except that it was a variation on the Cinderella theme. The heroine was a little girl, badly treated by a wicked mother and wicked sisters, starved, beaten. It was all very real to me. I pleaded with my mother to invite the girl home, give her a good dinner, comfort her. My mother couldn't convince me that it wasn't real, that the girl was an actress who didn't need a meal or comfort. I remember I wept because I wasn't allowed to protect her or help her.

It was something like that all over again. I felt needed. I wanted to protect Laura Malone, with my life if necessary. I wanted to touch her, to soothe her, to erase the look of tragedy in her dark blue eyes. I was out of my cotton-picking mind, but that's the way it was. Five minutes after I laid eyes on her I could have told you exactly how the gold-blonde hair curled down around her ears, just how the soft yielding mouth tightened at the corners when she was being decisive, just how a kind of desperate hunger was mirrored in her eyes when Drury was mentioned.

I understood now why Drury hadn't ever gone back to her after South America. I understood what he meant when he'd told Peter he couldn't see her because he might find himself forgetting what had happened to his family. "I need you!" is a siren song most of us can't resist.

She and I were alone in Chambrun's office. I'd called down to the grill and talked to Mr. Quiller, the captain there. He would have a table facing the entrance for Peter. I gave him a quick sketch of the situation. Then I called Cardoza in the Blue Lagoon. Laura was not to be discouraged from having a drink there by herself. If she was approached by anyone, Cardoza was to hold his fire until he got some sort of signal from the girl that she was in trouble.

I came away from the phone and offered her a drink.

"It looks as if it might be a drinking evening," she said. "I think I'd better save up for it." She suddenly lifted her hands to her face. "I—I sometimes think I don't want to find Neil, don't want to see him," she said.

68

"Why?"

"Because he won't be the Neil I know."

"His changed face?"

"Not that." She lowered her hands and her eyes were brimming with tears. "Five years of hating. Five years of scheming and plotting. Five years without love, without loving. I listened to Mr. Chambrun just now and I wondered if I was wrong. Maybe I won't know him because he's no longer the man I knew. He can be so changed inside that nothing will come across to me."

"If Chambrun's right that may not matter. He'll come to you."

"And if I don't know him?" She looked up at me, her eyes wide.

"He'll be pleased. It'll mean his disguise is perfect—if you don't know him."

"Oh, God!"

"What is he like?" I asked. Chambrun had said we had to know everything there was to know about him.

She was silent for a moment. "Somebody is bound to have told you about me," she said. "That I was a professional sex peddler when I met Neil."

I felt my jaw muscles tighten. "Peter told me. How you met Drury, went to live with him, were on the verge of marrying him."

"We were married," she said, "except for a legal document." She turned the dark blue eyes on me, and my knees weakened. "You're only the second man who knows about me who hasn't looked at me as though I was a freak. Neil was the other. Maybe Peter, because he knows that Neil loved me, doesn't think I'm all bad."

I said something meaningless because I didn't know what to say.

"You're wondering how a girl comes around to selling

her talent in bed to make a living."

"I wasn't wondering because I don't think I really want to know."

"You're wondering if I've gone back to it—without Neil."

"Have you?"

She turned her face away. "There can never be anyone for me until I see Neil, face to face, and he tells me he never wants to have me again."

"Doesn't five years tell you anything?"

"Only that he loves me too much to place me in the position of losing him twice."

"A sort of Sir Galahad?" Because of being moonstruck I actually resented a man I'd never met, knew nothing about.

She looked at me and she saw what it was.

"I'm asking about him," I said defensively, "because Chambrun feels we need to know everything we possibly can about him—to help us find him."

"Will it help you to find him if I tell you that he was a man of enormous good humor; a realist, unhampered by phony anxieties and guilts; a happy man, good at his profession, good at his relationships with people; a man without vanity. Will any of that help you to spot him, Mark?"

"No—except that Chambrun may be right. Drury won't let you run the risk of being used by Chang. He'll want you out of here. You should do as Chambrun said—run, as far and as fast as you can."

"Neil will have to tell me that," she said.

I knew she couldn't be argued out of it. "When did you last see him, actually?" I asked her.

A look of pain came into her eyes. "We'd been together for almost a year. A wonderful year. I—I'd finally given in; promised I'd marry him. He had to go to New York to do some location shots on a film. When he came back there'd be a few days shooting to finish the film and then we'd be married and go, he promised, on a three months' holiday to any place that occurred to us on the spur of the moment. There was no hurry about getting married. After all, we were living together as a man and wife live together. He wanted the legal trimmings; they didn't matter to me." She closed her eyes for a moment as if to shut away pain. "He came back from New York in high spirits. He'd seen Peter, his best friend, and his family and told them all about me. But all! Nobody had tried to lecture him. He'd had to tell them because somebody else would have passed on the word about me, surely. The final shooting of the film was going to take less time than he'd thought. In a week we'd be off—to the moon, if we chose. Then, in the middle of the night, the phone rang. It was the news from Buenos Aires. Some idiot gave him the gruesome details then and there. I didn't know it, but I'd seen Neil—my Neil—for the last time the night before."

"You literally never saw him again?"

"I saw him off at the airport that morning. I might as well not have been there. He'd turned to stone."

"You never saw him again?"

"No."

"He didn't get in touch with you?"

"Not directly. David Tolliver, his agent, called me. He'd made money arrangements for me. Months later there was a phone call from Peter Williams." Her lips trembled. "At first I was hurt more than you can imagine. Surely, when he got back here to this country, he'd call me on the phone. He didn't, and eventually I understood it. If he talked to me, if we got together once more, I might divert him from the only thing that mattered to him now—revenge."

"And that's exactly what you want to do now—divert him."

"Yes."

The office door opened and Miss Ruysdale looked in. "Mr. Williams is established in the grill," she said.

"So it's my turn," Laura said.

"If there's anything—any message, any contact—get to a phone and call me," I said. "The switchboard will know where to find me."

She reached out and touched my hand with cold fingers. "Thank you, Mark."

I watched Laura go. I went over to Chambrun's sideboard and poured myself a drink.

"Don't get yourself hurt," Ruysdale's voice said behind me. She was standing in the doorway, a small, wry smile moving her lips.

"Nobody's gunning for me," I said, and swallowed a stiff jolt of Jack Daniels.

"You can get hurt by other things than guns," Ruysdale said. "She's a fascinating girl."

I turned away because I didn't want her to see how close she was to being on target.

"She isn't going to come your way, Mark," Ruysdale said. "She's waited five years for Drury. You don't come across that kind of total devotion very often. Charming as you are, Mark, you're not going to be the least bit tempting to that girl. Forget about it. Do your job. Help to see that she doesn't get hurt, but don't start imagining that she's going to be a gold ring that'll come your way in the end."

"I know that," I said, stupidly angry at being mothered.

"I hope you do, Mark. It came over you in a hurry. Get over it in a hurry."

I went down the hall to my rooms. I changed into a dinner jacket with a soft shirt, my uniform for evenings in the hotel. I took time to call Mrs. Kiley, the switchboard supervisor, to tell her I would be down on the main floor. If either Peter or Laura called she was to find me at once.

Then I went downstairs. I collared Mike Maggio, the night bell captain. I gave him a special assignment. He was to keep Laura in sight for as long as she was moving around the hotel. I took him over to the entrance to the Blue Lagoon. Mr. Cardoza, the maître d', was standing just beyond the red velvet rope that shut people out of the room till Cardoza gave his okay.

Laura was sitting at the bar, a drink in front of her. She was turned sideways on a stool facing us. She showed a nice expanse of leg. She looked directly at us, and I might have been a total stranger. There wasn't a flicker of recognition. Maybe Drury had taught her to be an actress.

"She's already had her first proposition," Cardoza said.

"Who?"

There were three men sitting together at a far table. I knew them all by sight, part of the Madison Avenue crowd that came in often.

"The three of them suggested she join them for dinner," Cardoza said.

Just then a man came over from a far end of the room and stood beside Laura. He spoke to her, very tentatively, not pressing. She looked at him, smiled, and shook her head. This one I didn't know. He was about the right height, slim, not unattractive. By a weird coincidence Marty Miller, who plays a nice piano between the main shows in the Blue Lagoon, was making a nice thing of "Love, Your Magic Spell Is Everywhere."

"English actor, playing in a show at the Plymouth Theater," Cardoza said. "He checks out."

"It won't be hard to keep an eye on her," Mike Maggio said. "She's quite a dish."

I turned and walked across the lobby to the grill room. Peter had been given a table in the center of the room. The black goggles appeared to be aimed directly at me, but of course he didn't know I was there.

"Ordered a big dinner," Mr. Quiller, the captain, told me. "But he's just toying with it. Doesn't seem to have much of an appetite."

I could imagine. Peter was obviously straining to hear a voice, a familiar voice; hoping to be seen, hoping suddenly to feel a hand on his shoulder and words that would identify Drury for him.

Jerry Dodd materialized from somewhere.

"You're needed," he told me. "The Chang cavalcade is about to arrive and the boss is still upstairs looking for bombs. You're to be the official greeter."

That wasn't a new job for me. I'd often stood in for Chambrun in this capacity. If the guest is important he is met, welcomed, asked if there is anything special he needs. Then I go up to his room with him to make certain everything is in order there. So I was about to meet Drury's Chinese butcher.

You could feel the tension mounting in the lobby. The "sore thumb" cops and agents had been alerted and you could tell they were waiting for something important. I looked down the corridor toward the main entrance and saw the first of half a dozen Cadillac limousines arrive. Out of it came two men in business suits, obviously cops or agents, and two Chinese. The Chinese were big, imposing men like the late Li Sung. They came quickly along the corridor between the brightly lighted shops. Wexler and Larch appeared from somewhere and held a brief conference with the four men. One of the Chinese seemed to be the most vocal, making what looked to be angry gestures. Orders were passed. Eight or ten of the casual men in the lobby suddenly took positions along the corridor in front of the shops.

The second Cadillac pulled up in front of the door.

Men materialized outside the hotel and surrounded this second car. First out of it came two more of this giant breed of Chinese, these two in uniform. Behind them, also in uniform with rather gaudy red trim, was General Chang. Like the four other Chinese I had seen, he was a big man, powerful shoulders, hands like hams encased in white gloves. I was reminded of Li Sung's high cheekbones, square jaw, wide cruel mouth. I am not only not an expert, I know absolutely nothing about different Chinese ethnical groups —where you'd expect to find big men and small men. The Chinese I had encountered in my life had been mostly in city restaurants, and a pleasant little guy who did my laundry when I first came to New York to live and work. I didn't know then where these giant-type Chinese came from. I've since been told Mongolia.

Chang came through the revolving door, paused inside for his four giant bodyguards to flank him, then he strode toward the lobby, the other cops and agents falling in behind him.

In the lobby, press cameras and one TV camera had materialized. One little guy with a camera ran forward asking the General to "hold it there for a moment, please, General." One of the giant Chinese guards took him by the back of his coat collar and literally heaved him out of the way.

They were descending on the desk where I was waiting to greet the General, Wexler and Larch standing just to one side of me. They bore down on us, striding so quickly that some of the rear guard were trotting to keep up with them.

Chang was like something in a nightmare—or perhaps that may have been an afterthought—as he came closer. The huge yellow face was carved out of rock, the mouth a wide gash, the eyes narrowed slits. The face seemed to grow larger and larger, like something on film with the camera zooming in for a closeup. I stepped forward, wearing my professional smile of welcome—and that is all I remember until I emerged from some kind of agonized darkness and heard Doctor Partridge, the house physician, saying in his gravelly voice: "The sonofabitch could have killed him!"

It seems the first of the Chinese guards had hit me, with a stiff forearm, directly across my throat, a backhanded blow that had knocked me flat on my back and out cold. Chang, without breaking stride, had swept on to the elevators.

So much for the official greeting from the management of the top luxury hotel in the world.

CHAPTER 3

My eyes felt as if they were going to explode out of my head. I was lying on the examination table of the small first-aid room back of the reception desk on the main floor. Dr. Partridge, smelling of Sen-Sen, was bending over me. It was his theory that Sen-Sen would obliterate the smell of sour-mash whiskey, which he started drinking in the late afternoon in the Spartan Bar, where he played a nightly game of backgammon with some of his cronies. The sour mash would have smelled better to me.

"Just hold still, Mark," he said.

I realized my tie had been undone and my shirt collar was open. I tried to speak and felt an unbearable pain in my throat.

"Karate-type chop," Doc said. "Could kill a man."

Then I saw he was talking to Chambrun, a Chambrun whose face showed a concern for me that made me feel good. It seemed he cared. I tried pushing myself up on my elbows. The pain centered in my throat and at the back of my head. It developed I'd struck my head against one of the pillars in front of the desk when I went down.

"If you hold still, boy, I'll give you something to ease the pain," Doc said. "Not much else I can do."

I tried speaking. It came out as if I had a severe case of laryngitis, a wheezy whisper.

Chambrun reached out and gave me a little pat on the shoulder. "You had us scared for a while, Mark. Would you guess that you've been out cold for about twenty minutes?"

"What happened?" I asked.

"One of Chang's men," Chambrun said. "He wasn't prepared for you to step forward. They're all uptight as hell. The General, by phone, has offered his apologies, but after all, you could have been an assassin."

"How come they weren't prepared?"

Chambrun's eyes narrowed. "They had been told," he said. "It was a public performance to show the world how tight the security is. If it hadn't been you, it would have been someone else. Pictures of what happened to you will be in tomorrow's papers and on the television newscasts."

I swung my feet over the edge of the table and sat up. I wished to God it had been somebody else. "Take over like gangsters, you said. Jesus!" I touched my throat, gingerly. The room did a couple of loops around me and then settled down. That was when I saw Peter standing over by the door.

He looked very pale. I suppose there had been a big to-do in the lobby and that the word had circulated. Had it gotten to Laura, I wondered. I wished she'd turned up to worry about me. That's the kind of idiot I was. Then I realized that the excitement in the lobby would have given Drury a good chance to approach her, unnoticed. She wasn't the kind of person to desert her post.

One thing had been demonstrated. It wasn't going to be easy to get close to Chang. Maybe I'd been lucky. Chang's boy could have chosen to shoot me down in cold blood.

"Maybe we should just abandon ship and let him have the hotel," I said to Chambrun.

There was cold anger there. "If I have to I can play his kind of game in spades," Chambrun said. "Right now I'm concerned about you."

"I'm okay," I said. "Anything happen for you, Peter?"

Peter shook his head. "Nothing. Complete blank there. When I heard what had happened to you I decided to come over. What about Laura?"

"Just before Chang arrived she was in the Blue Lagoon, attracting males like flies," I said. "Mike Maggio's keeping an eye on her."

"Neil probably saw the whole thing," Peter said.

"If he did he knows what he's up against," Chambrun said.

The door behind Peter opened and Wexler came in, sucking on an empty pipe. He gave me a tired smile. "Glad to see you've come out if it, Mark."

"No thanks to the forces of law and order," I said.

"Don't be bitter," he said. "When you're up to it the General wants to express his regrets in person."

"Screw the General," I said.

Wexler turned to Chambrun, still smiling his tired smile. "The General wants to see you at once, Mr. Chambrun. He made it an order. I simply convey the words to you. He wants to tell you exactly how the routines must be set up for him."

Chambrun didn't answer.

"He also wants you to help him plan a birthday party," Wexler said.

"He *what?*"

"The day after tomorrow is his birthday," Wexler said. "He proposes to give a rather large party—several hundred people. He wants you to know just what he wants. There isn't much time, he tells me, for fresh salmon to be flown in from the West Coast."

I have, in the course of my duties at the Beaumont, rubbed elbows, you might say, with some of the most important men —and women—of our time. We have entertained royalty; provided living quarters for prime ministers and ambassadors; worked out itineraries for great writers, painters, musicians, actors, and directors; the industrial giants of our day, the world's top bankers, have lived with us and been served by us. Some of these people were great humanitarians, great personalities. Some of them were villains. All of them were a little larger than life size.

This is a preamble to saying that I had never come face to face with anyone who gave the impression of such enormous, raw power as General Chang. I couldn't guess his age, but whatever it was, it was his prime of life. His four personal bodyguards were big men, but I had the feeling Chang could have taken them all on at once and wiped up with them. Whatever his excesses might be they didn't include any sort of physical dissipation. I had expected a kind of manic arrogance, but, so help me, in the privacy of his own quarters he had a special charm that was almost winning. I had to remind myself of a man downstairs with his eyes gouged out, and another man, somewhere close by, whose mother and sister had been ravaged and murdered and whose father had begged for mercy for his family until he was silenced by a burst from a machine gun.

I had persuaded Chambrun to take me up to the twelfth floor with him to discuss—for God sake—General Chang's birthday. We got an immediate taste of twelfth-floor security. At the lobby level one of Jerry's men, an FBI agent, and a small Chinese gentleman were posted. Elevator number two had been removed from general use, reserved only for people going to or from Chang's corridor. Jerry's man and the FBI boy gave the all clear sign on us, but it wasn't good enough for Chang's man. Every detail about us had to go down in a small notebook before we were allowed into the elevator. The operator was a stranger to me; he must belong either to Wexler or to Larch.

"No problems?" Chambrun asked as this man started the car up.

"You're the first not connected with the security to go up, Mr. Chambrun."

And we got the full treatment. At the mouth of Chang's corridor two men sat in the chairs we'd supplied, sub-machine guns resting in their laps. They stood up, instantly, covering us. One had a little lapel-microphone attached to his coat and he spoke into it. The first door on the right opened and Larch appeared, his face deadpan.

"Pierre Chambrun, the hotel manager, and Mark Haskell, hotel public relations," he said.

One of the machine gunners nodded. "Will you face the wall, gentlemen, and put your hands behind your heads. Just routine."

We were frisked like gangsters who had just robbed a bank.

"You're going to search every bellboy and waiter in this fashion?" Chambrun asked.

"Everyone," Larch said.

"The General is going to eat a lot of cold food," Chambrun said.

"He's expecting you," Larch said. "This way."

He took us to the door of Chang's suite and pressed the door buzzer. "Stand to one side," he suggested. I thought I saw a nerve twitch high up on his cheek.

The door opened, fully blocked by two of the Chinese giants, each with a drawn handgun. One of them was the boy who had slugged me.

"Mr. Chambrun and Mr. Haskell," Larch said.

A small voice from behind the two giants said: "They may be admitted."

The armed giants stepped aside so that Chambrun and I could squeeze past them, single file. We went through the foyer. A small Chinese, obviously the owner of the small voice, gave us a ceremonial bow and waved us toward the living room. He wore a frock coat.

No two suites in the Beaumont are furnished alike. This one seemed rather out of place for Chang's oriental splendor. It was early American, the furniture starkly simple, hooked rugs on the polished floors, the paintings on the walls American primitives.

The geography of the suite consisted of the small foyer we'd come through, this large living room with windows looking out toward the East River, the glass rectangle of the United Nations building visible; beyond it, I knew, were two bedrooms, two baths, and a small service kitchenette.

I saw it only subconsciously, because Chang faced us in the center of the room, a wide smile on that face carved out of yellow marble. He had removed his uniform tunic and replaced it with a magnificently embroidered silk dressing gown, its colors brilliant.

"Mr. Chambrun." A slight inclination of the head, quite Western. "Mr. Haskell." The smile remained as if it was painted on. The eyes seemed to blaze. He gestured toward a delicately beautiful Chinese girl who stood in a far corner of the room. "My secretary, Miss Taku."

She lowered her head in a tiny bow.

"Please be seated, gentlemen." The General waved at two comfortable armchairs.

"I prefer to take my orders standing, General," Chambrun said.

Chang's eyebrows rose. "Orders? My dear fellow, I have asked you to come here to help me, not to give you orders." His English was perfect, without a trace of any accent I could place, unless it was slightly British. "Miss Taku can provide you with tea, or, if you prefer, we seem to have a well-stocked American bar."

"Nothing," Chambrun said.

The General's shoulders moved in a slight shrug, as if to imply that he had done his best to be courteous. "I owe you an apology, Mr. Haskell." The smile faded. "Perhaps you can understand that my personal safety comes first with me. I had supposed that Mr. Chambrun's hotel would be a safe place for me to stay in New York. I had supposed that your government agencies would have made it totally safe. Yet my top man, my close and trusted friend Li Sung, was murdered in cold blood when he came in advance to check out the preparations. It became evident to me that I could only rely on my own forces to keep me safe. When you suddenly stepped in my path in the lobby, Mr. Haskell, Yuan Yushan acted instinctively, and quite properly from his point of view."

I turned to see if Yuan Yushan was still standing behind

me with a drawn gun, but the two giants had evidently stayed out in the foyer.

"You were told in advance that you would be greeted in the lobby," Chambrun said.

"By you, Mr. Chambrun. By you. I had no reason to suppose an underling would take your place. When a strange man stepped forward—" He shrugged. "You are both aware that there is a maniac somewhere nearby who has only one aim in life, to kill me. You know that we have no way of guessing what he looks like. So we will take no chances. Let anyone, no matter who, make any sort of unexpected move toward me and I will not wait for you, or Mr. Wexler, or Mr. Larch to try to explain to me. Explanations will be worthless if Neil Drury manages to get to me. So you see, from where I sit, Mr. Chambrun, anyone may be Neil Drury unless he is well checked in advance and I know exactly why he is near me. Do I make myself clear?"

"Quite."

"And while we are on this painful subject," the General went on, "I find myself distressed by the information that you are offering your hospitality to two people who are obviously my enemies."

"What two people?" Chambrun asked.

"Laura Malone and Peter Williams," Chang said. "Mr. Wexler has offered me a rather absurd explanation for this. These people, he naïvely assures me, are here to help you identify Neil Drury so that you can persuade him to let me alone. You take me for a child, Mr. Chambrun?"

"Anything but," Chambrun said. His voice was colorless.

"Williams and Miss Malone are Drury's closest and dearest friends. They have no other interest but to help him. In addition, Williams, who is under the delusion that I was responsible for what happened to Drury's family in South

America and therefore what happened to him, is just as eager to get at me as Drury is. I would qualify as a patient for a mental institution if I allowed myself to believe that these two people are concerned with anything but to see me destroyed. Therefore, unless you want their deaths on your conscience, Mr. Chambrun, I urge you to get them out of the hotel and as far away from it as possible—tonight, at once."

"Is that also Mr. Wexler's wish?"

"Mr. Wexler's wishes are no concern of mine. Your people put on the masks of politeness and efficiency, but deep down, to use your American slang, they hate my guts. I must protect myself, Mr. Chambrun."

"Wexler must have expressed himself about Miss Malone and Williams," Chambrun said. "He believes, as I do, that whatever their feelings are about you their concern is to keep Drury alive. Whatever Wexler or Larch or Mr. Foster feel about you, General, their job is to keep Drury from getting to you. To do that, they must spot him. Miss Malone and Williams are their best bet."

"It is your decision to make, not mine," Chang said. "I shall protect myself."

"Wexler told you they were here so that you would not misunderstand why they were here," Chambrun said.

Chang's wide smile reappeared. "Mr. Wexler did not tell me they were here," he said. "I told him! That's when he gave me this naïve explanation."

"How did you know they were here?" Chambrun asked.

"My dear Mr. Chambrun, you don't really suppose that I am only protected by my bodyguards and my staff who have arrived here with me, and by the lamented Li Sung who came a day ahead of time? There have been people in your hotel for some days, watching, watching."

"Who?" Chambrun asked.

"If I told you that, Mr. Chambrun, my defenses would be only half as effective." He laughed, softly. "And now to the main reason for your being here." He made a gesture to Miss Taku, who came forward with several sheets of paper in her hands which she held out to Chambrun. He took them, frowning.

"As Mr. Wexler has told you," Chang said, "the day after tomorrow is my birthday. I choose to make a diplomatic function of it. That is a list of people I plan to invite —most of them from the diplomatic corps at the United Nations. Diplomats and their families."

"Most of them?" Chambrun asked, still scowling at the lists.

"A few persons not connected with politics," Chang said.

Chambrun looked up, his eyes widened. "Laura Malone? Peter Williams?"

Chang chuckled. "If they are still alive the day after tomorrow I would prefer to have them where I can see them rather than snooping around behind my back. Also, there are always gatecrashers at a party like this. I suspect Neil Drury will make a try at it."

"And how will a gatecrasher get by our guards out in the hall?

"Mr. Chambrun, you are not thinking clearly. There are over two hundred names on that list. The party cannot possibly be held up here. I'm told the Grand Ballroom is the only facility that would be adequate."

"If you wanted to commit suicide, this would seem to me to be an admirable way to arrange it," Chambrun said.

"I think it may be a perfect way to dispose of my enemies," Chang said. "Reveal them and dispose of them."

"The Grand Ballroom is not available on that day,"

Chambrun said.

I happen to know that it was.

"Then make it available," Chang said. "I'm quite certain the State Department will urge you to make it available. Now, I would like to talk to you and your banquet manager about food, drink, some sort of music and entertainment to go with the evening."

"There isn't time to arrange such a party," Chambrun said. "Wexler mentioned special salmon from the Northwest. It would take days—"

"I'm told you are a magician at arranging such things in an emergency," Chang said.

The little man in the frock coat emerged from the foyer. He bowed apologetically to Chambrun and me and then spoke to the General in what I suppose was Chinese. The General frowned.

"It seems I must answer questions from a Lieutenant Hardy, a homicide detective. He is concerned about Li Sung."

"A first-class man," Chambrun said.

"But a waste of time," Chang said. "We all know who killed Sung, but I choose to deal with him in my own way, with my own methods."

For the first time Chambrun's voice took on an edge. "By gouging out his eyes?" he asked.

Chang's mouth tightened, and then he laughed. "You are still believing in the myth that I had anything to do with the Drury tragedy in South America. I assure you that *is* a myth, Mr. Chambrun. How soon can we discuss plans with your banquet manager?"

"Mr. Amato has gone home for the night," Chambrun said. "If I can reach him, he can be back here within an hour."

"Make the effort." Chang said. "Let me know when you are ready to talk."

We were dismissed.

CHAPTER 4

There were a lot of scary things about the situation, but I think what disturbed me most was that Chambrun seemed to be caught off balance. He was not in total control of his world. Chang was making the rules, an unheard-of situation in the Beaumont. The General's diplomatic status was, in effect, giving him a license to kill. You couldn't hold the law over his head as a deterrent. He had a right to protect himself. If an innocent person got caught in the meat chopper, the General could give his shoulders an Oriental shrug and point to the fact that all the king's horses and all the king's men had failed to put a known assassin under lock and key. While an unidentified Drury was on the loose, Chang could justify almost any violence.

"If our President was in the same position in some foreign city, we'd expect the Secret Service to protect him," Chambrun said when we were back in his office. "If a strange man suddenly pulled a gun out of his pocket, we wouldn't expect the President's guards to wait for the local gendarmes to serve a warrant."

Chambrun rarely drinks, but on that occasion he went to the sideboard and poured himself a generous three fingers of cognac. When he brought it back to his desk, he seemed to be more interested in inhaling it than drinking it, the little snifter glass cradled in his two hands.

"He'll use Drury as an excuse to tackle Drury's friends," I said, "Peter and Laura in particular."

Chambrun raised his heavy lids to look at me over the rim of his glass. "I noticed that the lady threw you a little off center, Mark."

I think I actually blushed. It was so absurd, when you thought of it. I hadn't had more than three minutes of private words with her. "Both of their lives have been wrecked by Chang," I said. "So I feel protective. Is that so childish?"

"Your protective impulses do you credit, but don't get burned," Chambrun said.

"Look," I said, "we've got to locate Drury. We've got to get him away from here and talk sense to him. We've got to make it clear to him that he's not only risking his own life but also his friends' lives."

"I had a thought on our way here," Chambrun said. "Rather, I had thoughts. The first of them was that I have been an idiot. We are dealing with a ruthless master of political intrigue in Chang. Of course he wouldn't depend on Wexler, or Larch, or Foster to protect him. Of course he would have had someone here well in advance to scout out the situation. More. It's not only the hotel they'd be interested in, but the UN, the city streets, the car-rental agencies they use, every item of service they'll require. He wouldn't count on our official people or even his own. He's got someone looking over Wexler's shoulder. Sung knew about Peter Williams and Miss Malone. They weren't a surprise to him. He's ahead of us every step of the way." He took a tiny sip of his brandy. "We have four men on a list, one of whom we thought might be Drury in disguise. One of them could equally well be Chang's man. For all we know they have already spotted Drury, are waiting for him to make his move. And if he doesn't move soon enough for them this absurd birthday party may tempt him. It may occur to Drury that Chang's birthday should also be his deathday."

"We have to find him!" I said.

"Do we have a chance without Williams and Miss Malone to help us?"

"But they—"

"We have to use them and try to protect them at the same time," Chambrun said. "So far they've only talked to you in generalities, Mark—what his voice sounds like, his characteristic gestures. We need to know him much better than that. We need to know him as intimately as though we were married to him, which, in effect, Miss Malone was." He smiled. "And since you feel so protective, I think you're the one to dig it out of her."

"So when she tells me what he was like in bed, where are we?" I asked.

"We may get to know how we can trap him into revealing himself. And we have to find that out in a very great hurry, Mark."

"Had you thought he, too, might have an advance man here in the hotel?" I asked.

"Good boy," Chambrun said. "Now you're starting to think about something besides Miss Malone's sad blue eyes."

A little red light blinked on Chambrun's desk and he switched on the intercom. "Yes, Ruysdale?"

"Johnny Thacker is here with a package for you," Miss Ruysdale's voice informed him.

"Package?"

"From General Chang."

"Send him in and come with him," Chambrun said.

Johnny was wearing the dark blue coat with brass buttons and a pocket patch with the word "Beaumont" sewn in gold thread to it. He was carrying a small, square package wrapped in ordinary brown paper.

"He sent for me and Wexler told me to go up," Johnny said to Chambrun. "I went through the mill up there. Jesus. Frisked, fondled by both cops and robbers. I was finally let into the presence. Did you get a look at that Chinese chick, Miss Taku? I'd like to find out personally if it's true what they say about Chinese women."

"To the point, please, Johnny," Chambrun said.

"His Majesty was there, all smiles, holding this package in his hand. Would I convey it to you? Would I be sure to hand it to you in person? Not to Wexler or anyone else. Just to you. It's my job to say yes to everyone, so I took it."

"And Wexler?"

"He's waiting with his tongue hanging out for you to call him and tell him what it is. He held it up to his ear for a while before he let me bring it. I guess he thought it might be a bomb."

Chambrun took the package and opened it, slowly and quite carefully. Inside the brown paper was some tissue paper. Inside the tissue paper was a small tape recorder. Chambrun's face was a study.

"The General wants me to know," he said, "that his room is no longer bugged." He switched on the recorder and the tape wound soundlessly. If anything had been recorded, it was now erased.

"I forgot to tell you," Johnny said. "The General said you should know he was disappointed to find you playing children's games with him."

I went back down to the lobby. If anything my concern for Laura—and Peter, of course—was more intense. You saw Chang in action, you listened to him, and any doubts you had that he could be as big a monster as he'd been painted disappeared. Laura and Peter were pawns in the game that he'd wipe off the board without thinking twice, use with complete ruthlessness if it would help him get to Drury and end that threat forever.

I went directly to the Blue Lagoon. The room was crowded now, with a dozen couples waiting hopefully outside the velvet rope for a table.

Laura was no longer at the bar.

"She moved on about a half hour ago," Cardoza told me.

"To where?"

Cardoza shrugged. "Maggio was floating around in the distance. He'll know."

"Nothing happened here?"

"She probably has a few bruises from being pinched," Cardoza said. He gestured toward the far end of the room. "Your other pigeon is here."

I'd been too concerned about Laura to notice Peter at a corner table, staring blankly toward us.

I went looking for Mike Maggio and found him lounging over by the newstand, talking to the redheaded gal who manned it until it closed about one o'clock.

"Watching your chick got me feeling hungry," he said, giving the redhead a wink.

"Where is she?" I asked.

He waved toward the door of the grill room. "Doing her thing in there," he said.

"Don't lose her."

I went over to check. Laura was sitting at the bar again. She saw me, for sure, but she gave no sign of it. God knows if Drury was looking for her she stood out like a neon sign.

I needed to talk to someone, so I went back to the Blue Lagoon and joined Peter at his table. He seemed glad to see me.

"I hoped you might catch up with me," he said. "This

listening bit in a public room like this isn't going to work, I'm afraid—unless Neil wants it to happen. Is that birthday party for real?"

"For real," I said. "Would it surprise you to know that you and Laura are on his guest list?"

The black goggles jerked my way.

"We need to face some very hard facts, Peter," I said. "Chang doesn't believe for an instant that you and Laura are here to turn Drury off. He thinks you're here to help Drury, so you're the enemy. You're invited to the party because he wants to be able to keep an eye on you. Make one slightly suspicious move in the General's direction—pow!"

"And he can get away with it?" Peter asked.

"He can get away with it. I know you and Laura feel you must stay here, hoping to make a contact with Drury. I know that is our best chance to find him. But I still think you both should get as far away from here as you can and stay there till this is over."

"Till they kill Neil," Peter said, his voice harsh.

"He's calculated his own risks. He doesn't want you to share them or he'd have approached you long ago. If Chang decides to use you or Laura against him, you'll have spoiled his only chance of succeeding.

Peter's right hand gripped the cane that was hooked over the arm of his chair. "If I had the slightest notion that Neil could succeed with what he has in mind, I'd do what you say; go away and let him work it out by himself. But he can't succeed, can he?"

"Very small chance," I said. "At best he may get Chang and be torn to pieces. More likely he'll be killed before he can get anywhere near the General."

"Killed by Chang's men, or even our own people if they try to stop him and he won't be taken."

"True."

The black goggles turned away. "Chambrun could be right, you know. Chang could try to grab Laura—or both of us—as hostages. But Neil might not make a move to prevent it, or help us after it happened."

"He loves you both," I said.

"He did love us both," Peter said. "Laura was his whole life for a year. Now revenge is his life. He might not lift a finger to help either of us."

"You're saying he's stopped being a human being; become a revenge-crazy maniac," I said.

"I'd have to talk to him to know for sure," Peter said. "But if he has, no man alive could blame him." His voice was low and unsteady. "The last thing I ever saw in this life was what happened to his mother, his sister, and his father. Would you be surprised if I told you that the first thing I remember every morning when I wake up is that scene? Would you believe that I go to bed with it in the front of my consciousness, like a bloody film run over and over for my benefit? I hear a sound, or smell an odor, in the course of a day and it comes back—the sight of those filthy bastards defiling Mrs. Drury and Joanne—lovely Joanne. I hear Mr. Drury screaming for mercy, not for himself but for them. I can see the giant Mongolian butcher who led those men watching, laughing. His face is always part of that nightmare, bearing down on me, his knife glittering in the sunlight!" Peter raised his hand and brought it down on the table so hard my glass and his coffee cup bounced and slopped over. People sitting near us turned to look, shocked by the violence of it.

"You say it was Chang," I said. "He says he was never there—said it to us tonight."

Peter drew a deep breath, fighting for control. "I heard of Chang when I first arrived at the embassy in Buenos Aires. There was a great deal of talk about Cuban and Red

Chinese revolutionaries who were training and drilling antigovernment forces in the mountains. Chang was a big name, often talked about. The man I saw, the chief butcher, matched descriptions of Chang that have since been given me. I—I've never been able to look at a picture of him. If he was sitting at this table with us I'd have no way of being sure he was the man who blinded me."

"His voice? Wouldn't you know his voice?"

"I don't think so. That time was bedlam. A hundred men, laughing, shouting, cheering as they—they fouled and killed the women. When the leader came to me, ready to blind me, he shouted his orders to me at the top of his lungs so that everyone could hear. I never heard him speak a conversational word. It—it's all a blurred madhouse of sound."

"So it was only assumptions by the press and political people down there that identified him as Chang?"

"My description of him seemed to confirm it for them."

"And what did he look like?" I asked, trying to make it sound very casual.

A nerve twitched near the edge of the black glasses. "A big man—over six feet—the biggest Chinese I'd ever seen. High cheekbones, a pasted-on smile. Broad, broad shoulders. Cold eyes, like pieces of cut glass." Peter reached out and his hand closed over my wrist. I almost cried out, the grip was so painful. "Is that man upstairs, Mark?"

"He could be," I said. "But there are four other men up there, Chang's bodyguards, who might fit that description. Li Sung would have fit it."

Peter loosed his hold on my wrist. "What does it matter whether it was Chang himself, or one of his men, trained and ordered by him?" Little beads of sweat had sprung out on his forehead. I found myself wondering what would happen if Peter found himself alone with the General. Neil

Drury couldn't hate him any more than Peter did.

"I know what you're thinking, Mark," he said. "That I hate Chang, that I'd like to destroy him." He laughed a jangling sound. "Yes, I do; yes, I would. But for me it would not be just enough for him to die. I'd want him exposed. I'd want him tried for murder before the whole world. I'd want proof of his guilt, not just the pleasure of breaking his neck. I'd want the world to know the kind of man we're sucking up to, inviting into our councils, treating with abject public courtesy. I wish I could persuade Neil that he's wrong; that there must be a way between us to get at the truth and make it public."

"For that he has to be found," I said. My drink was gone and I signaled to the waiter for another. I told Peter about the check we'd done on registered guests at the Beaumont, and that we'd only come up with four we couldn't pretty well account for. I ran them down for him. There was Robert Zabielski, five feet eight, overweight, involved with a hooker who'd spent the last two nights with him in his room drinking sour-mash bourbon.

"Neil is my height, almost six feet," Peter said. "He couldn't shrink himself."

I went on to Paul Wells, apparently about seventy. Right height, right weight, wrong age, genuinely bald. Peter shook his head.

Next there was Sam Schwartz, the phony Hollywood impresario. Right height, right weight, an ugly scar on his face that could be the result of clumsy surgery. Big talker, big roll.

"It's a part Neil could play," Peter said.

Finally there was James Gregory, the emphysema victim with the oxygen tank. Dr. Partridge testified the illness was genuine.

"He checks out in a way," I told Peter, "but there is an odd coincidence. His doctor, a man named Coughlin, is known to us. Good customer of the hotel's. But he happens to be a plastic surgeon, not a specialist in lung diseases. He explained to Doc Partridge that Gregory is an old friend; he's caring for him because of that friendship. All the same, our man Dodd wondered if Coughlin might be the surgeon who altered Drury's face."

"Interesting possibility."

"Which brings me to a question, Peter," I said. "Foster, the State Department man, told us he 'understood' Drury had undergone cosmetic surgery. He knows Drury and he assumes he wouldn't know him if he sat down next to him. You and Laura accept surgery as a fact. How did you come to know about it? You haven't had any contact with Drury you say."

"It was in the newspapers when Neil got into trouble in the East three years ago," Peter said.

"How did the newspapers get it?"

"Some journalist in Hong Kong helped Neil get away," Peter said. "He gave out the story. His name was Rattigan, a Reuter's correspondent. He was immediately transferred from the area. Chang made it unsafe for him."

"Where is he now?"

Peter shook his head. "I tried to locate him to get the whole story from him. According to Reuter's he walked out on his job after he was transferred—to Europe. He seems to have disappeared into thin air. I've never been able to get on his trail."

"Chang?" I suggested.

Peter's mouth tightened. "Could be," he said.

I saw Mr. Cardoza, the maître d', coming toward us. "You and Mr. Williams are wanted in Mr. Chambrun's office," he told me. "Lieutenant Hardy has some questions to ask you."

Peter and I walked out of the Blue Lagoon into the lobby, his hand resting gently on my arm. I saw Mike Maggio, still trying to make time with the redhead at the newsstand. He signaled to me that Laura was still in the grill.

Lieutenant Hardy, the homicide man, is, I think I've said, an old friend of ours at the Beaumont. He is a big blond man who looks more like a professional fullback than a modern cop. The key to his success over the years is his thoroughness. He's not a fireworks kid, but he covers every inch of a territory he's concerned with and he talks to everyone remotely concerned, and he keeps at it and at it until the pieces of his puzzle fall into place.

Over the years Hardy and Chambrun, temperamentally as different as two men can be, have developed a genuine mutual respect. Working together they are a very tough team. Chambrun's impatience is complemented by Hardy's dogged, detailed, and very thorough checking; Hardy's plodding tempo is picked up by Chambrun's often brilliant improvisations.

Miss Ruysdale was still on the job when Peter and I got to the office and she gave us the green light to go on in. Chambrun was slumped in his desk chair, smoking, the inevitable cup of Turkish coffee in front of him. Hardy, his tie loosened, the top button of his white shirt undone, was having a very thick corned beef sandwich, washing it down with a glass of beer.

Without any direction from me, Peter walked to one of the armchairs as though he could see it and sat down.

"No luck downstairs, Mr. Williams?" Chambrun asked.

Peter shook his head. "He could be ten feet away and I wouldn't know it unless I heard him speak."

"You don't believe in Miss Malone's extra-sensory perceptions?"

"I want to," Peter said, "so part of the time I believe in it and part of the time I don't. No bells have rung for her so far."

"She's still circulating downstairs," I said.

Chambrun frowned, but he didn't say anything.

Hardy wiped his mouth with a napkin and pushed his plate away. The sandwich was gone, down to the last crumb.

"I feel like an outsider," he said. "You people are not very interested in my problem."

"Wrong," Chambrun said. "If, as seems likely, Neil Drury is your murderer we're very interested."

Hardy took a notebook out of his pocket. "I've got nothing here that indicates anything—yet," he said. He looked at me. I sensed he was a little embarrassed by Peter's blindness. "You two are the only ones I've found so far who had any direct contact with my corpse. Seems strange that nobody noticed a large Chinese guy circulating around the hotel."

"Not so strange," Chambrun said. "To begin with, those of us who were alerted to trouble did not expect General Chang and his party to arrive until tomorrow. You know this hotel, Hardy. It's a center for UN people—Indians, Japanese, Chinese, Mexicans, Puerto Ricans; any race and color you can think of. Simply the fact that he was a large Chinese wouldn't have brought Li Sung any special notice here."

"He hadn't registered," Hardy said. "He wasn't a guest of the hotel."

"He was on the list of people in General Chang's party, due tomorrow."

"The point is, nobody seems to have paid any attention to him when he showed up here earlier today."

"I repeat, no reason why anyone should." Chambrun's impatience was beginning to show. "You expect the doorman to telephone my office every time a foreigner walks through the revolving door?"

"So Mr. Sung was as commonplace around here as ham and eggs," Hardy said, unruffled. "The point is, I don't know when he got here, how long he'd been hanging around. General Chang, through his interpreter, tells me he got to New York last night."

Chambrun leaned forward. "Interpreter?" He laughed. "General Chang speaks better English than you or I!"

Hardy laughed. "So he was putting me on." He made a note in his book. "Now, Mark, you and Mr. Williams actually talked to Li Sung. Tell me how it was."

"I had brought Peter here to the hotel and moved him into my apartment," I said. "I came down here to report to the boss."

"What time was that?"

"Late afternoon," I said. "I didn't make a note of the time. But wait a minute. Wexler was here, and when he left this office he said something about our having twenty-two hours to get things organized. Chang was due to arrive at Kennedy at three o'clock tomorrow. That would have made it somewhere around five o'clock."

"So let's get on to Li Sung," Hardy said.

"Mr. Chambrun and Jerry Dodd and I talked for a few minutes after Wexler left. Then I went down the hall to rejoin Peter and found Li Sung with him."

"Right around five o'clock?"

"Right. Maybe nearer five-thirty."

Hardy made a note. "So you were the first one to see Li Sung, Mr. Williams." Hardy looked up, frowning. "I beg your pardon, Mr. Williams. I meant to say—"

"Don't be embarrassed, Lieutenant. The word 'see' is an acceptable figure of speech. It doesn't hurt me."

"Sorry."

"Forget it. I was alone in Mark's apartment. I'd been taking up the time he was gone with learning my way around. A routine I have to go through if I'm going to stay in the place. The door buzzer sounded and I crossed the room, pleased that I could make it without bumping into something, and opened the door. I was aware that someone was facing me, but I couldn't guess who. 'Yes?' I said. A half-amused voice said, 'Man, you must be Peter Williams.' Young sounding, American sounding. But some instinct told me this wasn't a friend. I'd left this stick of mine hanging over the back of a chair in the middle of the room. I turned my back on the man in the doorway and I felt a hell of a lot better when I reached out and found my stick. I was perfectly oriented. I moved around the chair so that it was between me and my caller. He laughed. 'That's cool,' he said. 'The way you handle yourself is cool.' I assumed, whoever he was, he was looking for Mark. I told him Mark was down the hall in Mr. Chambrun's office. 'No sweat, Dad,' he said. 'I was looking for you.' "

"How could he expect to find you there?" Hardy asked. "Had you registered?"

"I don't think so," Peter said. "I mean, I don't know if Mark had registered for me. I didn't register."

"He wasn't officially registered," I said. "Atterbury the reservation clerk, knew he was sharing with me. Johnny Thacker, the day bell captain knew. I told him on my way up, asked him to make himself useful to Peter. So if Li Sung asked the right person he might have found out."

Hardy scowled at his notebook. "He didn't ask Atterbury or Thacker. He didn't ask the switchboard."

"The switchboard hadn't been notified," I said.

"But he didn't ask. He didn't ask anyone we've checked with," Hardy said. "So how did he know?"

Chambrun's coffee cup made a clicking noise in its saucer. "We're beginning to think that someone we haven't spotted was here in the hotel as an advance man for General Chang," he said. "Li Sung would have known—could have asked him. The man, whoever he is, could have seen Mark take Mr. Williams upstairs; could even have overheard him talking to Johnny Thacker."

"It'll do for now," Hardy said. "So what did Sung want from you, Mr. Williams?"

"He wanted me to leave the hotel. 'I order you to leave the hotel, man,' he said. He made it quite clear. I was a friend of Neil Drury's, so I was a potential enemy of Chang's." Peter's mouth hardened. "I also have my own reasons for being Chang's enemy, 'Although you're wrong, man, in thinking he had anything to do with what happened to you.' He told me if I made any kind of a wrong move they wouldn't wait to ask me questions. Just then, Mark came back."

Hardy looked at me.

"He repeated all that to me," I said. "And he included Laura Malone in his threat. He knew that Wexler was producing her from the West Coast."

"How did he know that?"

"He didn't say. He knew."

"So then what?"

"He left, after Peter tried to tell him he was only here to persuade Drury to give up. Sung told him he could 'tell that to the marines.' "

"Then what?"

"Peter and I talked for a while—about Li Sung, and about Miss Malone. Then I came back here to report to the boss what had happened."

"Know the time?"

"I remember looking at my watch as I came down the hall. Six-thirty."

"And then?"

"We went up to the twelfth floor to check out the arrangements that had been made for Chang's party."

"And then?"

"I rejoined Peter. He was listening to the seven o'clock news, I remember. We decided to go down to the Trapeze for a drink. While we were there Jerry Dodd came to tell us that Li Sung was spread out on the sidewalk outside the hotel."

Hardy studied his notebook. "Li Sung left your room a little after six. You talked till six-thirty. You returned here and went back to your room while the seven o'clock news was on. You went down to the Trapeze where Jerry found you."

"Right."

"Li Sung went off the roof at a few minutes before seven," Hardy said. "Must have been while you were here talking to Mr. Chambrun."

"Why didn't we know at once?" I asked.

Hardy shrugged. "A cab driver saw the body hit the street. He wasn't sure where it had come from. He called the cops from a drugstore on the north side of the hotel. It has a street entrance, you know. This cabbie didn't come into the hotel. A patrol car was on the scene in five minutes. But it was probably ten minutes before they let Jerry Dodd know what had happened. It looked as though Sung had taken his dive from the hotel. Routines took time. Jerry had things to do before he came looking for you. The point of interest is that Sung lived less than an hour after he left your apartment, Mark. And I have a question. What the hell was he doing on the roof of the hotel outside Mrs. Haven's penthouse?"

Nobody made a guess because Mike Maggio came into the office followed by Miss Ruysdale. Mike looked more serious than I had ever seen him.

"I'm sorry, Mr. Haskell," he said to me, "but I lost her."

Believe it or not, I didn't follow him.

"Miss Malone," he said. "I lost her. She was in the Trapeze, having a drink for herself. I—I had to go to the john. I figured she was settled for a moment. When I came back she was gone. Mr. Del Greco said she just signed her check and walked out. Nothing unusual about it, he said."

"You tried her room?" Chambrun asked, his voice sharp.

"She's not there," Mike said.

Chambrun was on his feet. "Let's get moving," he said.

Part Three

CHAPTER 1

Maybe the security should have been tighter. All she'd planned to do was move around in the public rooms on the chance that she might "feel" Drury's presence. Mike Maggio is a sharp and dependable guy. I'd felt perfectly safe as long as he was keeping an eye on her. I thought it was understood that if she saw anything, "felt" anything, she'd call me at the switchboard. Nobody was going to use any muscle on her out in public with Mike Maggio at the ready and the whole hotel swarming with cops and special agents.

She couldn't walk from one room to another without interested and protective eyes being aware of her. And yet she had.

In the first few minutes of our hunt for her I wasn't really worried. We'd pick up her trail the minute we began checking with the cops, the agents, and with Jerry Dodd's people. I should have known that Mike Maggio wouldn't have come to Chambrun's office in an obvious panic unless he'd first made exactly that kind of check. He hadn't just stood in the lobby holding up a wet finger to see where the wind was coming from. He'd checked, and then he'd come at once to Chambrun, the right thing to do.

"You phoned her room?" Chambrun asked on the way

down to the lobby. We used the stairway, not waiting for an elevator. Peter was walking beside me, his hand gripping my arm.

"Phoned," Mike said. "When she didn't answer, I had the housekeeper go in with a passkey. She wasn't there; nothing upset."

When we reached the lobby Johnny Thacker joined us. As I've explained, he was doing an extra duty.

"Nothing so far," he reported. "She isn't in any of the bars, the private dining rooms, the ballroom. The drugstore is the only shop open. Not there. One thing is certain, nobody dragged her out of the Trapeze by force. She'd have yelled, wouldn't she?"

"She might, she might not," Chambrun said.

"She knew the hotel was filled with people who'd help her if she lifted a finger," I said.

Chambrun looked at me, his eyes two glittering little slits. "Would she lift a finger if she spotted Drury?" he asked. "She knew there were people around who would help her, but she also knew that there was someone—or maybe several some-ones—working for Chang who would also be watching. She wouldn't want to give Drury away to them."

"If she spotted Neil," Peter said, his voice harsh, "she'd try to get to talk to him alone, no matter what the risk. You're right, Mr. Chambrun, she wouldn't want to betray him to Chang's people."

We stood there, looking around the lobby, as if, somehow, it would provide us with answers. The traffic was reasonably light. I spotted at least eight people I knew belonged to Wexler and Larch.

"What happened after we came upstairs, Mike?" I asked.

"She came out of the grill," Mike said. "She'd been there quite a while. I took her on a brief tour of the places that were busy—back to the Blue Lagoon where she'd been earlier, a brief look into the Spartan Bar, which had its usual quota of old gents playing cards and backgammon, to the Grand Ballroom where there's a coming-out party in progress, mostly young people. Finally I told her the Trapeze would begin to fill up when people started coming back from the theater. So we went up there and Del Greco got her a table facing the entrance. She ordered a vermouth on crushed ice. 'I'll stay here for a while,' she told me. So—so I had to go to the john and I went."

"How long were you gone?" Chambrun asked.

"Not five minutes," Mike said. "When I came back she was gone. She hadn't touched her drink, according to Del Greco. She called him, said she'd changed her mind, signed her check and went out."

The Trapeze is at the mezzanine level. There are two ways to get to it or leave it. You can go up in an elevator to the mezzanine. Cars in the north bank of elevators open up right opposite the entrance to the Trapeze. You can also use a wide flight of stairs that come straight down into the lobby, open stairs that are visible from top to bottom. If she'd used the elevator she could go up or down. If she used the stairway she could only have gone down into the lobby where a dozen people would have been instantly aware of any trouble. The elevators have operators on them till midnight. After that they go on to a self-service system. There had been operators on them when Laura left the Trapeze. Mike had already questioned them.

"She's a nice-looking chick," Mike said, "but she wasn't wearing anything flashy; a plain black dress and a black patent-leather handbag, gloves. Her blonde hair was pretty outstanding. But with heavy traffic on the elevators she wouldn't have attracted any particular attention. Still, that blonde hair is noticeable. None of the operators on the north cars remembered seeing her."

I found myself wondering how anyone could see her and not remember.

Chambrun gave orders. A general alarm was to be spread, Wexler and Larch notified; there should be a search of the hotel from penthouses to the basement. Doormen should be questioned hard. If she had left the hotel one of them might have gotten her a taxi.

"I want all of you to keep in touch with me each step of the way," Chambrun said. "Don't save it up for a surprise."

He and Peter and I went up to the Trapeze. Everything looked perfectly normal there—normal for the Trapeze, that is. As I've said, you'll see more famous and notorious people there than most places, mainly because there is no gawking public to interfere with them. They can be unselfconscious there. They seem to wear sort of social masks without any cracks in them. The women tend to be expensively put together, dressed, jeweled. You'll see more different hair colors than God ever invented.

No one, except Mr. Del Greco, seemed to be aware of us when we arrived and stood at the entrance. The patrons of the Trapeze are exempt from any such vulgarity as curiosity.

"No news, sir?" Del Greco asked.

Chambrun shook his head. "Tell me about her leaving here."

"There was nothing odd about it," Del Greco said. "She'd ordered a drink and then she changed her mind. Like someone who'd forgotten an appointment and suddenly remembered it."

"She seem nervous—frightened?"

"Nothing like that. She beckoned to me and I came over. 'I've changed my mind,' she said. At that moment the waiter produced her drink. She said she'd sign for it. I said it wasn't necessary if she wasn't going to drink it. She said she'd ordered it and she'd sign for it. The waiter handed her the check and she signed—Laura Malone, room seven-o-seven."

"Did she seem in a hurry?"

"Not exactly," Del Greco said. "She'd decided not to stay. She paid her bill—tip added, by the way. She said thank you and walked out."

"Did she seem anxious to get out of here before Mike came back from the men's room?"

"It didn't occur to me at the time. It was no kind of a scrambling exit."

"How closely were you watching her after she came in?"

"Not closely," Del Greco said. "I watched everybody, as you know." An explanation of why the service was so expert in the Trapeze. "Mike hadn't gotten around to telling me who she was then. 'Look out for the lady,' was all he said. 'She's a friend of the Great Man's.'" Del Greco's mouth repressed a smile. "Meaning you, sir. She asked for a table facing the door and I managed to find her one. She ordered a drink. Mike went to the men's room. Then she changed her mind."

"Did you have the impression she'd seen someone here she knew, perhaps wanted to get away from?"

"I had no reason to think that. As I said, she'd made up her mind to go, but there was nothing hysterical or panicky about it."

"No one spoke to her or signaled to her?"

"Not that I saw."

"If she should come back, report to me at once."

"Of course."

A feeling of cold anxiety was creeping over me. I'd been so sure she'd get to me if anything special happened. Yet Del

Greco made it seem that nothing had happened to disturb her or frighten her. She'd play it cool, I thought. If she'd seen someone here in the Trapeze, if she'd persuaded herself that someone was Drury, she'd play it very cool. But why not get in touch with me or Peter at once? Why disappear?

Chambrun and Peter and I, Peter's arm on mine, walked down the stairs to the lobby. I think we all felt a little lost. A search was under way, but what did we do next? Just sit and wait for someone to report something positive?

Johnny Thacker joined us. "No telephone calls in or out of her room," he said. "Neither doorman remembers seeing her. Lots of people come and go, of course, and they had no reason to be watching for her."

I felt Peter's fingers tighten on my arm. "Chang," he said, in a very low voice.

"She can't have been spirited up there," Chambrun said. "They'd have to get her by Larch's and Wexler's people."

"They wouldn't have to take her there," Peter said. "You said you thought Chang had people in other places in the hotel."

"She seemed to leave the Trapeze of her own volition," Chambrun said. "Nobody spoke to her or signaled to her, according to Del Greco."

"He could have missed it," Peter said. "Someone could have walked by her table and dropped a note. It could have happened. It could have happened earlier in the Blue Lagoon."

"Why would she walk, wide-eyed, into a trap?" Chambrun said. "She isn't a fool. She was aware of the danger."

"If she was told where she could find Neil—that Neil was in trouble," Peter said. "Chang will know, if they used that to trap her."

"And Chang will not tell us," Chambrun said. He started

toward the elevators.

"Where to?" I asked.

"Chang," he said. "It's worth a try."

We went up in the isolated elevator to the twelfth floor. Chambrun had ordered Peter to wait in my rooms, with one of Jerry Dodd's men to protect him. Peter, his hand shaking on my arm, insisted he be allowed to go with us.

"Nothing can happen to me with you there," he said. "Chang knows I'm in the hotel. *I want to hear him speak!*"

It made sense. The old question, denied by the General, as to whether he had commanded the butchers in South America might be answered.

Submachine guns were pointed at us from the mouth of the corridor on twelve. The man with the lapel mike reported us and Wexler came out of the first room. He needed a shave.

"You crazy?" he said, looking at Peter.

"It's worth a try," Chambrun said.

"He can refuse to see you," Wexler said. "All or one of you."

"I don't think he'll refuse to see Williams," Chambrun said. "That's why I let him come. Chang will be too curious."

"I'll try him, but I doubt if he'll agree," Wexler said.

"Tell him if he says 'No' there'll be no room service," Chambrun said. There was a tiny smile at the corners of his mouth.

"You couldn't do that," Wexler said.

The smile widened. "If my help went on strike even God couldn't do anything about it," he said.

"Let me try without threats," Wexler said. He was a very tired man as he walked down the hall to the door of Chang's suite.

The familiar routine took place. Yuan Yushan and his giant friend stood in the doorway, handguns drawn. We couldn't hear what Wexler said or what the reply was from inside. It took a long time. Then Wexler came back.

"You were right," he said, sounding surprised. "If you'll face the wall and lock your hands behind your heads—"

We were very efficiently searched and the little Chinese guard wrote down our names in his notebook. And then we walked to the door, between Yushan and his friend. Peter's hand on my arm shook so I thought he was suffering from a chill. The little man in the frock coat gave us his oriental bow and we were facing General Chang. The General's eyes were bright with a kind of excitement.

"You are full of surprises, Mr. Chambrun," he said.

Peter's fingers bit into the flesh of my arm. The General's eyes were fixed on him.

"We are meeting sooner than I expected, Mr. Williams," he said. The wide smile widened. "Shall I keep on talking? I expect you are listening for a voice you heard some years back. Do I sound familiar to you, Mr. Williams?"

I looked at Peter. A little trickle of sweat was running down his face past the black goggles. He didn't speak.

"But you didn't come here just to introduce me to Mr. Williams, did you, Mr. Chambrun? You are concerned about the disappearance of my other enemy, Miss Malone."

"Your intelligence department is highly efficient, General," Chambrun said.

"The very best," Chang said. "It has to be. Just imagine. A country which dreams itself to be the most powerful in the world, unable to reach out and put its hands on one miserable, revenge-crazed maniac. Thousands and thousands of dollars spent to pay the salaries of guards who are not certain they can guard. The top man in my entourage murdered in cold blood, and neither the Federal Government nor the city police able to make an arrest. One reformed prostitute able to disappear from a crowded area of this hotel, ringed around by so-called security agents. Do you wonder, Mr. Chambrun, that I must depend on my own intelligence and security forces?"

Chambrun's smile was cold. "If that is a true analysis of the situation, General, then it will be clear to you why I come to you to ask what has become of Miss Malone. Your people should be able to help me where my fumbling staff has failed."

"Oh, that's rather good," Chang said, laughing softly. "Very good. Unfortunately I do not, as yet, have a report from my people. They are, of course, only concerned that Miss Malone and her killer boyfriend do not get anywhere near me. If they should, after we have dealt with them I'll be happy to let you know where to find them. As for Mr. Williams—have you decided yet, Mr. Williams, whether mine is a voice you've heard before? In any event, I've allowed you to come in here with Mr. Chambrun, so that you'll know if you try getting to me without my permission you will find yourself very stone-dead. Since you can't see, has Chambrun described to you just how tight the security is? Are you aware of the two men with automatic rifles out in the hall? Are you aware of the two men who are standing just behind you with drawn pistols? Are you aware—and are you, Mr. Chambrun—that every move you make in the hotel is being watched by men you couldn't see, even if you had eyes?"

"It is those men who can tell us where Miss Malone is," Chambrun said, dangerously quiet.

The smile faded from Chang's face. "I find myself bored by this absurd exchange, Mr. Chambrun."

"I, too," Chambrun said. "What it amounts to, General, is a declaration of war between you and me."

Chang laughed again. "A declaration of war between a hotel manager and the Republic of China? Because in my role here, Mr. Chambrun, I am the Republic of China. Your President, your State Department, your Justice Department, your Secret Service are committed to protecting me. Are you taking them on, too, Mr. Chambrun?"

"I can try," Chambrun said. "I know I can make your stay here so unpleasant that you will beg to be housed somewhere else."

"Try, and you will be removed from your job in the space of time that it takes me to make a phone call to Washington."

"So we know where we stand," Chambrun said. "I recommend that you help to see that Miss Malone is returned unharmed, immediately. If not, we'll both discover what I can do against the Republic of China. Good evening, General."

"Couple of silly kids, swapping threats!" Chambrun said, as we walked down the corridor to the elevators. " 'My father can lick your father.' " It wasn't until we were out of earshot of the guards at the mouth of the corridor that he spoke to Peter. "Well, Mr. Williams?"

Peter had given up any pretense of operating by himself. He was hanging onto my arm as though I were a life preserver. He still had violent shakes and his face was wet with sweat.

"So help me God, I don't know," he said. "He's so suave, so smooth. My man—my voice—was shouting." He shook his head. "You could see him, I couldn't. Do you think he knows about Laura?"

"He likes to play games," Chambrun said. "He likes to

wave his power like a flag. But he's a perfectly normal man in one respect."

"How?" I asked.

"He doesn't want to die," Chambrun said. "Drury is a real danger to him, Mr. Williams is a danger, and Miss Malone. Anyone connected with Neil Drury is a danger. If he doesn't know where Miss Malone is, he's just as interested in finding her as we are. If he does know where she is—"

"He'll use her to force Neil into the open, or at least hold his fire," Peter said.

The elevator door opened and we went into the car. The operator, one of Jerry's men, asked: "Any luck?"

Chambrun shook his head.

At the lobby level the car door opened and Jerry Dodd was facing us. "Just coming up to find you. We've got something—maybe."

We stepped out of the car.

"The drugstore," Jerry said. He didn't stop to explain but started walking briskly across the lobby toward the drugstore, which is located next to the side-street entrance to the lobby.

There are half a dozen shops in the lobby area, all but one of them lining the corridor that leads in from the Fifth Avenue entrance—a gift shop, a bookstore, a furrier, a jeweler, a women's dress shop. You can enter those shops only from the corridor. But the drugstore, across the lobby by the side-street entrance, has a door into it from the lobby and it also has a door opening directly out onto the street. You don't have to come into the hotel to enter the drugstore, and you don't have to come into the lobby to get out onto the street.

The night manager of the drugstore, an Armenian named Kervorkian, was waiting impatiently to close up for the night. Understand, the shops aren't run by the hotel. We just rent space to these businesses.

"Tell Mr. Chambrun what you told me," Jerry said to Kervorkian.

Kervorkian was a pharmacist. Normally he handled only the filling of prescriptions, or the sale of nonprescription drugs. A clerk or clerks handled the doodads—the toothpastes, the Alka-Seltzers. Sometimes Kervorkian got kind hearted and let the clerks go home a little before closing time. He'd done that tonight. He had been alone in the shop for the last forty-five minutes.

"I was just checking out the cash register when this girl came in," Kervorkian said. "Nothing specially to notice about her except her hair—kind of a gold-blonde. I paid attention only because we sell all kinds of junk for coloring hair—shampoos, rinses. I wondered if it was real, and if it wasn't what she used. That was all."

"What time was it?" Jerry prompted him.

"About a quarter to twelve," Kervorkian said. "I was planning to close a few minutes early if there wasn't any traffic. Been a dead evening."

The time fitted.

"What did she want?" Chambrun asked.

"A forty-eight cent tin of aspirin," Kervorkian said. "I remember because I'd locked up the money in the cash box, ready to take it inside to be put in the safe, and I made change for her out of my own pocket."

The drugstore management had an arrangement with the hotel to leave its night cash in our care.

"This girl was alone?" Chambrun asked. "Nobody waiting for her by the door, or outside on the street?"

"I didn't notice anyone, but I wasn't looking for anything, you understand. I was anxious to close up and I followed her

118

to the door and locked it when she went out."

"The door to the lobby?"

"No, Mr. Chambrun, the door to the street. She went out onto the street."

"Did anyone meet her there? Did you see her take a cab?"

"I just didn't pay attention," Kervorkian said. "There was no reason I should. I wanted to close up."

Jerry looked at Chambrun. "Could be," he said.

"And there are half a million blondes in New York City," Chambrun said. "Still, the time is right—"

It could have been Laura. The distance from the foot of the stairway coming down from the Trapeze to the lobby door into the drugstore wasn't more than fifteen yards. Unless she called attention to herself by being in too much of a hurry there would have been no reason for the cops or Jerry's men to pay special attention. They were looking for Drury, not Laura. She was free to come and go as she chose. A visit to the drugstore wouldn't seem abnormal.

Peter and I went back to Chambrun's office with him. Reports were beginning to come in from a small army of searchers, all negative. Chambrun wanted to be where he could be found. Jerry had stayed behind to check with cab drivers who waited in a hack stand outside the side-street entrance. The blonde with the tin of aspirin might just have taken a cab, might just be remembered.

Peter sat in one of the big leather armchairs, his hands raised to his face. He was emotionally done in. Miss Ruysdale had produced a tray of sandwiches and some American coffee. No one wanted to eat, but the coffee tasted good. Ruysdale stayed with us. She'd evidently gotten a high sign from Chambrun.

"If the blonde in the drugstore was Miss Malone, she wasn't dragged there by force, or out onto the street by force,"

Chambrun said, really talking to himself. He was at his desk. "What you suggested, Williams, could have happened. A note dropped on her table which Del Greco didn't notice, something before that in the Blue Lagoon or the grill. Drury, or someone from Drury, arranging a rendezvous outside the hotel."

"She knows what a dither we'd be in which I didn't find her—when Mike didn't find her," I said.

"Nothing would matter to her if she thought she was going to see Neil," Peter said.

"When you men get into a situation like this you can't think of anything but melodrama," Miss Ruysdale said in her cool, matter-of-fact voice. "The girl is under enormous pressure. What seems normal to you and Mark, Mr. Chambrun, might get to be a little hard to take—the endless hum of conversation around her, the clatter of dishes, the sound of music coming from the Blue Lagoon and the ballroom. All of that is a normal and happy sounding part of your everyday world."

"Dishes do not 'clatter' in the Beaumont," Chambrun said, but he was listening.

"She's thinking about her man, the danger he's in, the violence he's planning," Ruysdale said, ignoring the comment. "She may simply have decided she wanted to get a little fresh air. The aspirin suggests she had a headache. A little fresh air, a walk, a chance to think about her next move. She hadn't 'felt' Drury was anywhere near. No one had told her she couldn't step out for some air, had they?"

"Not in so many words," I said. "We took it for granted she wouldn't get lost without letting us know."

"She could have walked from here to Poughkeepsie by now," Chambrun said.

"I didn't suggest that no one saw her go, that nothing has

happened to her," Miss Ruysdale said. "What I'm suggesting is that she left the hotel of her own free will, with nothing more in mind than a walk. She wouldn't feel obligated to let you know she was going out for five or ten minutes, Mark."

"She should have told Mike, shouldn't she?"

"He was there to protect her from wolves. He'd walked out on her," Miss Ruysdale said. "He probably didn't tell her he was just going to the john. So she went out to get a dozen breaths of fresh air."

"In New York City?" I said.

"Take your complaints to the Mayor," Miss Ruysdale said. "My point is that things could have happened to her that have nothing to do with Neil Drury or General Chang. She can have been hit by a car crossing the street; she can have been mugged by some hophead looking for money for a fix. There's more to the world, gentlemen, than the Hotel Beaumont, although you may not think so. Have you checked the hospitals? Have you checked with the desk sergeant at the local precinct house? If somebody snatched her purse a block away from here, she'd have no identification. You haven't put out a city-wide alarm, have you?"

Chambrun nodded. "You may have something, Ruysdale. Set it in motion."

Miss Ruysdale walked briskly out to her own office.

"She could be right, you know," Chambrun said. "She could simply have gone out for a walk. But I find it hard to buy a hit-and-run driver or a hash-hungry mugger. Our bright boys didn't pay any attention to her leaving, but there are others who would. Drury would. Chang's undercover boys would."

"In any case, Ruysdale's right," I said. "The outside world may be the place to look."

Peter made a moaning sound, his face still covered by his hands. "Let's hope to God it was Neil who saw her and followed her out," he said. "She'd be safe with him."

"Let's take a real tough look at it," Chambrun said. "Drury may not have been anywhere near the hotel tonight. All Chang's publicity informed the world he would be getting here tomorrow afternoon. Drury would know he couldn't find out very much about the arrangements being made to protect Chang until the General got here. He had no way of knowing that either Miss Malone or Mr. Williams was going to be in the hotel. He might decide it was risky to loiter around until showdown time came, because Wexler and Larch and their armies would be looking for him. So I say it's a better than even chance that Drury is somewhere getting a good night's sleep in preparation for tomorrow's action."

"So if he wasn't here, who killed Li Sung?" I asked.

"Some other enemy of the General's; a personal enemy of Li Sung's. Let's assume it, anyway, for the moment." Chambrun reached for his coffee cup. "But the General knew, early today, that Mr. Williams was in the hotel and that Miss Malone was due to arrive. Li Sung made that clear to you, didn't he?"

"That's one I can't figure," Peter said. "I didn't know myself I was coming to the hotel until a little before Li Sung came to Mark's room. How could he know about me? How could he know about Laura?"

"The General made it clear to us, didn't he, that there are 'eyes' in the hotel that see everything for him? Those eyes saw you arrive with Mark. What the General didn't say was that there are also 'ears' listening for him. Somebody leaked the fact to him that Wexler was bringing Miss Malone on from the coast. Li Sung knew. They were ready for her."

"What you're saying," Peter said, in a dead voice, "is that Chang knows where she went and why, and she'll be used to force Neil to reveal himself to give himself up to Chang!"

"That could very well be the name of the game," Chambrun said.

Peter turned his head from side to side, as though he was in pain. "You talked a hell of a big game of your own up there in the General's suite—about taking him on. How, in God's name?"

Chambrun glanced at the white face with its black goggles. "We'll have to find a way to put out his eyes and cut off his ears," he said. "That for a start."

CHAPTER 2

The Beaumont had always seemed like a wonderfully safe place to me. I have often described it as a small town, independent of the rest of the world, run by a highly efficient mayor in the person of Chambrun, with a first-class police force under the capable direction of Jerry Dodd. There was rarely any serious trouble, because Chambrun had a gift for anticipating it before it happened. It wasn't just a gift, come to think of it. It was marvelous organization. Nothing could happen in the Beaumont, from an explosion by a psychotic dishwasher in the kitchen to the love life of an African diplomat in the bridal suite, that Chambrun didn't know about within seconds. "When I don't know what's going on in my hotel it will be time for me to resign," I'd heard him say more than once.

That night, in his office, reports were coming to him directly and through Miss Ruysdale in a steady flow. They were reports that told him nothing helpful. For the first time in his life Chambrun wasn't in complete command of his world. Chang and his private espionage system knew more of what was going on in the Beaumont than Chambrun did. The rules of the game were laid down by Wexler and Larch —by the United States Government, in effect. Laura, under close watch by Chambrun's staff—me among them—had disappeared. Neil Drury, invisible to us, was planning a murder. There promised to be a head-on collison between Chang and Drury, and Chambrun was not in his customary position at the controls. While all this simmered, Chambrun was asked to make arrangements to have fresh salmon flown in from the West Coast for an arrogant birthday party. He had talked a "big game" to Chang, threatening to take on the Republic of China single handed. The truth was that, sitting there in his office with Peter and me, he didn't appear to have a single lead to any one of our problems—how to locate Neil Drury, how to find Laura, how to track down the roof-top murderer of Li Sung.

But lead or no lead, Pierre Chambrun was not a man to sit on his butt and wait for the world to come to an end.

"You still think your hearing is as sophisticated as you thought it was when you came here, Mr. Williams?" Chambrun asked.

"Would I know Neil's voice?"

"Yes."

"I think I would."

"There are four men in this hotel on whom we don't have a proper dossier," Chambrun said. "One of them just might be Drury. One or all of them just might be Chang's eyes and ears. There's no point in sitting here waiting for God to take a hand on our side. I want to talk to these men, and I want you to listen for some familiar vocal note, Peter."

Any kind of action did something to loosen the knots that had tightened, almost unbearably, in my gut. Whatever had happened to Laura—and thinking about it and knowing Chang was a terrifying business—I was partly responsible. I had been too casual about her "circulating." I had trusted someone else to do the watching. That wasn't entirely fair to Mike Maggio, because I would have trusted him with my own life.

Chambrun seemed to read my mind. "Don't blame yourself or Mike," he said, as he and Peter and I headed for the lobby. "If anyone had tried to drag Miss Malone out of the hotel against her will she'd have been covered. It's the one hopeful thing, as far as her safety is concerned. She chose to give you the slip."

"Unless she just went for a walk," I said.

"What happened to her after she walked out of the drugstore she may not have guessed was coming," Chambrun said. "But walking out would seem to have been her own choice."

Chambrun got the room numbers of our four possible "Drurys" from Karl Nevers, the desk clerk. He began with Robert Zabielski, the thirty-year-old salesman from Cleveland, who took a call girl to his room each night and did some solid drinking there. Room service reported that Zabielski had ordered two club sandwiches and a bottle of bourbon sent to his room, 509, about forty-five minutes ago. Mr. Del Greco in the Trapeze reported that Zabielski had been drinking there earlier with the same hooker who'd been his companion on the two previous nights.

"Mr. Zabielski is not going to be happy with me," Chambrun said. "Don't be surprised by my approach."

We went up to the fifth floor and rang the buzzer of 509. Nothing happened. I saw there was a DO NOT DISTURB sign hung on the outside doorknob. Chambrun pounded on the door with his fist.

"Open up in there," he shouted, "or I'll have to use a passkey."

There was a muffled "Wait a minute" from inside. Then the door opened as far as the inside chain would allow and we saw Zabielski's pale face. His hair looked rumpled. He was a scared cookie.

"What's the meaning of this?" he asked, with a show of bravado. "Can't you read the sign?" His voice was a husky croak and he seemed to have a little trouble breathing. His wide brown eyes were bloodshot.

"I'm sorry to disturb you, Mr. Zabielski," Chambrun said. "I'm the hotel manager. I'm sorry—"

"What are you, some kind of Christer?" Zabielski said. "I'll bet there are a hundred guys in this hotel who have a girl in their room. Why should you pick on me to—"

"I haven't any concern at the moment about the lady you're entertaining. There's been a bomb scare in the hotel," Chambrun said, blandly. "We have reason to believe it may have been planted on this floor, possibly in this room. I suggest you let us make a search for it unless you want to risk being blown to pieces."

There was a female squeal of terror from inside the room. The door closed a little and we heard the chain come off. Then we were inside. Chambrun gestured to me. I was evidently to search for the "bomb."

"What's it all about?" Zabielski asked, shaken. "Some kind of rad-lib on the loose?"

I glanced at Peter. He stood by the door, head cocked to one side, listening.

Zabielski was no Adonis. He'd pulled on a terrycloth robe but it didn't do much to hide his pot belly. A girl with platinum hair sat bolt upright in the bed, a sheet pulled up around her obviously naked body. On the bedside table was a half empty bottle of bourbon and two plates that had once carried sandwiches. I went through the motions of checking around the room and in the bathroom. I reported to Chambrun with a perfectly straight face.

"Seems to be all clear," I said.

"Sorry to have bothered you, Mr. Zabielski," Chambrun said.

We retired to the hall. We heard the chain go back into place. Chambrun glanced at Peter.

"Well, Peter?"

"Not possibly Neil," Peter said. "Wrong height, wrong size, wrong voice. Of course I have no way of telling whether or not he might be connected with Chang."

"Nor I," Chambrun said, his face grim. "So let's try number two."

Number two was Paul Wells, the bald, elderly gentleman with the rooming-house address in Philadelphia. He was not in 921, his room. When there was no answer to our knocking Chambrun did let himself in with a passkey. Mr. Wells was traveling light. There was one well-worn blue suit hanging in the closet. His supply of shirts, socks, and underthings was sparse. There were no letters or papers anywhere. The bathroom revealed the rather intimate fact that Mr. Wells had false teeth. If he was anyone's eyes or ears, the place was bare of any evidence to prove it.

We tracked him down, though. He was in the Spartan Bar, the no-women-allowed room that is a constant target for the militant feminists, but is still a haven for elderly woman-haters. Most of the patrons sit around talking about "the good old days," or playing chess, or backgammon, or gin rummy. It stays open until the last moment the liquor laws allow, because the old gents who gather there have nothing to go to bed for. Mr. Novotny, the Spartan's captain, pointed out Mr. Wells. He was sitting alone at a corner table, wearing an ancient dinner jacket, his bald head shining in the dim light.

"Been here since about ten o'clock," Novotny told us. "Hasn't left the table except to go to the men's room. Strange old boy. Talks to no one. Pays for each drink as he orders it, and he takes on quite a load without showing it. I meant to speak to you about him, Mr. Chambrun. I have the feeling he's spending his last bucks and that you may find him hanging from the chandelier in his room some morning."

Chambrun gestured to Peter and me to follow him. The old man looked up at us with vague interest in his faded eyes as we approached his table.

"I'm Pierre Chambrun, the Beaumont's manager, Mr. Wells," Chambrun said.

"It's a great pleasure to meet you, Mr. Chambrun," Wells said. He had a pleasant, cultivated voice. I looked at Peter, who was frowning, his head turned to one side.

"I just wanted to make sure you are enjoying your stay with us," Chambrun said. "This is Mr. Haskell, our public relations man, and Mr. Williams."

The old man gave us a courteous little nod. I saw a look of pity come into his face as he realized that Peter was blind.

"I'm honored, gentlemen," he said. "I've heard so much about you, Mr. Chambrun, it's a special pleasure."

"You have friends who know me?" Chambrun asked. It would be a way to check on the old boy.

"Oh, no," Wells said. "I—I don't have any friends here. But sitting here every night, as I have for the last week or so, I hear a lot of talk. You are very highly regarded, sir."

"That's nice to hear. If there is anything I can do to make your stay with us happier—?"

The old man allowed himself a gentle laugh. "I am dying of curiosity, Mr. Chambrun. I understand that earlier to-day—" He glanced at the clock behind the bar. "—really yesterday, now, isn't it?—a man was murdered, thrown off the roof? Have you—have the police—?" His voice trailed off.

"The police are being very closemouthed so far," Chambrun said.

"Which, in my experience, means they haven't come up with any certain answers yet." The old man made it a question.

"If they have, they haven't told me about it," Chambrun said.

"Of course you would be the first to know," Wells said.

"Pleasure to chat with you," Chambrun said. "Be sure and let me know if there's anything I can do to make you comfortable."

We all said good night. Out in the lobby Peter shook his head decisively. "No chance," he said.

"He's clearly not Drury," Chambrun said. "The age is genuine."

"He was pretty curious about Li Sung. If he is eyes and ears he could have been pumping you," I said.

"I wish I had answers for him," Chambrun said.

Jerry Dodd waylaid us on the way to the elevator to report—nothing. "The lady's gone, like smoke," he said. "Up the chimney. We've checked the cab stands. No driver on either side of the hotel remembers picking her up."

"Elevators?" Chambrun asked him.

Jerry made a wry face. "It was about the change over time to self-service, except on the Trapeze side. There were at least a half dozen cars without an operator that could have been used. You think she could have come back into the hotel without our seeing her? The whole place was alerted, boss."

"If she walked around the corner and came straight back in," Chambrun said. "Mike was only just starting to look for her and not too worried at that point."

"And gone where?" Jerry asked.

"If Drury did get a message to her—God knows where," Chambrun said. "We're checking out the four question marks, but Drury could have friends in the hotel."

Jerry looked at Peter's expressionless face. "How about that, Mr. Williams?"

"Of course there could be someone staying here who is a friend of Neil's," he said. "If you went over the guest list with me—"

"A thousand names!" Jerry said.

"Hollywood people, theater people," Peter said. "You could narrow it that much for a start. David Tolliver, Neil's agent, might be more useful than I—and quicker." He gestured toward the black goggles.

"An idea," Chambrun said. "Get hold of Tolliver, Jerry. Get him over here no matter how he bleats about the time of night. Have a guest list ready for him. Meanwhile we have our own special Hollywood character to see."

Sam Schwartz, our Hollywood phony, had a room on the fourth floor, one of our least expensive setups in spite of his "roll that would choke a horse."

"Listen carefully to this one," Chambrun said to Peter on the way up. "This one is reported to be the right height, the right weight, with a scar on his face that could be the result of bungled surgery, or could be clever makeup. This one could be Drury, Peter."

I saw a nerve twitch on Peter's cheek.

We left the elevator and went down the hall to 419. Chambrun rang the door buzzer. The door was ripped open so quickly it seemed Schwartz had been waiting for us. He faced us, a lithe, well-muscled, dark man, naked except for a pair of shorts. The ugly scar on his left cheek kept one corner of his mouth lifted in a perpetual sneer. God knows he was nothing like the pictures I'd seen of Drury in Tolliver's office.

"What the hell do you want?" he asked.

"I'm Pierre Chambrun. I'm the hotel—"

"I know who you are," Schwartz said. He glared at me and at Peter. "Who are your chums?"

Chambrun introduced us.

"So what's the gag?" Schwartz said. "You know what time of night it is? Waking up a guy at one-thirty in the morning!"

"Quite obviously you weren't asleep, Mr. Schwartz," Chambrun said. "You opened the door much too quickly. Were you expecting us?"

"How the hell could I be expecting you?"

"I wish I knew," Chambrun said.

"So speak your piece and get the hell out of here," Schwartz said, totally unembarrassed by his nakedness.

"I want to have a look in your room," Chambrun said.

"You got a search warrant?"

"I don't need one, Mr. Schwartz. I'm the final authority in the Beaumont. You are my guest. The fact is, there's been a bomb threat, and we're checking all the—"

"You think I've got some chick in here?" Schwartz

shouted.

"If you don't mind, I'll look," Chambrun said, and moved forward. I thought Schwartz was going to pop him, but he didn't. He backed into the room with us following him.

I did my phony search routine. Schwartz's closet was filled with mod sports clothes. There was nothing of any significance in the bathroom. No booze anywhere. There was a half empty pack of cigarettes on the bedside table, with a butt burning in the ashtray. Schwartz stood with his back to the bureau, as if to protect the key ring, the loose change, and the wad of bills that lay there.

"Well, Peter?" Chambrun asked.

Peter shook his head. "No, not this one," he said.

"Sorry to have bothered you, Mr. Schwartz," Chambrun said.

"You may be a lot sorrier in the morning," Schwartz said. "I'm gonna find out from my lawyer just what your rights are."

He slammed the door behind us as we went out into the hall. "He may not be Drury," Chambrun said, as we headed for the elevator, "but that was quite a performance. Just as sure as God he knew we were coming. Which makes him interesting."

We went back to the lobby and located Jerry once more. Chambrun picked up one of the house phones before he spoke to Jerry and talked to Mrs. Kiley, the night supervisor on the switchboard.

"Room four nineteen, Mrs. Kiley. I want his phone monitored."

"Jerry's had me on that room since earlier today," Mrs. Kiley said. I could hear her, standing next to Chambrun. "He's on the phone now."

"Inside call?"

"Outside, Mr. Chambrun. Murray Hill number." She rattled it off.

"You've got a girl on it?"

"Yes, sir."

"I'll hang on until she can report to us," Chambrun said. "Has he had any in-calls?"

"Just a minute . . . . Yes, sir. At one seventeen . . . . Call came from outside. Caller didn't identify himself. A man. He said: 'Schwartz? It's hit the fan!' . . . . Schwartz said 'Thank you,' and that was that."

"Thanks. I'll wait for word on this out-call," Chambrun said. He covered the mouthpiece with his hand. "You had Schwartz's phone covered, Jerry?"

"Right. And the three other guys we couldn't check out."

"Good man."

"The only call to or from any of the rooms was this one about twenty minutes ago. I figure Schwartz for a gambler, maybe horses. Somebody was telling him something went wrong."

"I wouldn't be surprised if I'm what hit the fan," Chambrun said. He took his hand from the mouthpiece. "Yes, Mrs. Kiley?"

"We have a tape of the call for you, Mr. Chambrun. I can give you the gist of it, if you like."

"Please."

"Four nineteen seems to have been talking to his lawyer, sir. He kept saying, 'You're my lawyer, aren't you?' He was trying to find out whether you had the right to search his room in the middle of the night, Mr. Chambrun."

"Only that?"

"That's it—couched in four letter words, sir."

Chambrun's smile was thin. "The lawyer's opinion?"

"A suit would cost him too much to make it worthwhile,

the lawyer said. The lawyer said you could probably stall him for two or three years before it got to trial."

"Thank you, Mrs. Kiley."

Chambrun put down the phone, frowning.

"Sounds as though he was really mad," I said.

"Or as if he knew his phone was monitored and he had to do something to make us forget the slip he made."

"What slip?"

"For God sake, Mark, he was waiting for us! 'It's hit the fan!' Someone warned him we were coming." He turned to Jerry. "I want Schwartz covered; his goings, his comings, his phone calls. The slightest thing out of order, shout."

"Right," Jerry said.

"I've got one more to cover; our friend with emphysema," Chambrun said. "After that I'll be in my office."

James Gregory had a two-room suite on the seventh floor —722. We were in for a surprise when we got there. The door was opened, after a decent interval of waiting, by a man who looked as far from being an invalid as anyone you could imagine. He was a tall, dark, athletically built fellow with a deep suntan. His eyes were brown, with little crow's-feet at the corners that looked as if they'd been etched there by good humor, not worry.

"Mr. Chambrun!" he said. "You probably don't know me by sight, but I've been a long-time customer of yours."

"Dr. Coughlin?" Chambrun asked.

So here was the plastic surgeon.

"How nice of you to put two and two together correctly," Coughlin said. "I suppose Dr. Partridge told you of me. I came into town to a medical dinner and party and thought I'd look in on my patient. Do come in."

We trooped in, and Chambrun made the introductions.

Coughlin looked at Peter with a sort of professional interest. "Dr. Partridge gave me some information about your problem here, Mr. Chambrun," he said. "He explained to me why you were interested in Jim—Jim Gregory, my patient. I must say I was surprised to find out how closely you check on your guests. I'd love to see what your file is on me—or would I?"

"Blue card, top drawer," Chambrun said.

"Well, that's comforting."

"We developed an interest in you, Doctor, because of your specialty."

"Plastic surgery? I can understand that since you're looking for a guy who has apparently had the full treatment. But sit down, gentlemen. Jim doesn't keep any liquor here. He doesn't drink. But I can make you some instant coffee in the kitchenette."

"No time, thank you, Doctor," Chambrun said. But he sat down and I guided Peter to a chair. "However, since we're here, Doctor, perhaps you can give us a little education on your specialty. Could you tell, just looking at a man who was sitting next to you, like me, whether he'd had a job done on his face?"

"Not if it was a good job," Coughlin said. "We're talking about some time after it was done, of course. There's a difference, though, between plastic surgery done to cover some physical damage, like the results of an accident or a wartime wound, and what we call cosmetic surgery. Where there's been damage to a face you have to work with what's there; you may have to restructure, difficult skin grafts. Surgery can be noticeable under those conditions, but it's better than having no nose, or no jaw. But you're really interested in your man Drury. He'd had no accident as far as you know?"

"No accident," Peter said.

Well, under those conditions cosmetic surgery is quite another story," Coughlin said. "I could change your Mr. Drury's face so that you wouldn't know him, his wife wouldn't know him, and another doctor wouldn't know he'd been worked on, unless he made a close physical examination."

"You could be Neil Drury and his girl wouldn't recognize him?" Chambrun asked.

Coughlin laughed. "Could be, if I fit other specifications; height, weight, other intimate details. She might know I was a fraud in bed." He turned serious. "It's much easier to say who *isn't* your Mr. Drury; not tall enough, too old, wrong voice. But, given similar vital statistics, I could fool his mother when I got through with him."

"With just small alterations?" Chambrun asked.

"That's what most cosmetic surgery is," the doctor said. "Straightening a nose, flattening out ears, removing some sort of blemish or birthmark. But I could change a patient totally if that's what's required; I could make him look like someone else."

"But you didn't," Chambrun said, casually.

"Drury?" Coughlin laughed again. "I read about him some years back when his family was exterminated. I suppose I may have seen him in a film. But I never met him; never heard the rumor he'd had his face changed till Dr. Partridge told me. The fact that the FBI, the CIA, his girl, his best friends, and General Chang's own agents haven't been able to spot him is a damned good advertisement for some unknown surgeon."

"He'd better keep it to himself until this is resolved," Chambrun said, "or General Chang might burn holes in his feet to get him to tell what Drury looks like now."

"It's a strange world," Coughlin said, frowning. "We shout our heads off about law and order, and at the same time we go all out to protect General Chang, a murderer."

"Rules of the game."

Coughlin nodded, slowly. "My job as a doctor is to keep people alive; as a plastic surgeon to make that life more bearable. I suppose if Chang had a bullet in his chest I'd remove it and fight for his recovery. Not very different rules, really."

"Your hand could slip and nobody would know."

"I'd know," Coughlin said. "I'd have to live with it."

The phone rang on a side table. Coughlin went over to it. "Dr. Coughlin here . . . . Yes, he is . . . . Yes, I'll tell him." He turned back to us. "Message for you, Mr. Chambrun," he said. "There's a Miss Malone waiting to see you in your office."

I felt my heart jam against my rib cage. I was on my feet and so were Chambrun and Peter.

"Thank you, Doctor," Chambrun said. "This is rather urgent."

We almost ran for the elevators, Peter hanging tight to my arm. We got off at the second floor and hurried down the hall to Chambrun's office. Miss Ruysdale was sitting at her desk in the outer office.

"She inside?" Chambrun asked, not waiting for an answer.

We barged into his private office.

It was empty.

"Where is she, Ruysdale," Chambrun shouted.

Miss Ruysdale had followed us, looking puzzled. "Where is who?" she asked.

"We just had a call saying Laura Malone was here."

"She hasn't been here, Mr. Chambrun. They found her?"

Chambrun, his face turned to stone, picked up the phone

on his desk. He pressed a button so that his conversation came through the squawk box. We could all hear it.

"Mrs. Kiley? Chambrun here."

"Yes, sir?"

"You put a call through for me in seven twenty-two a few minutes ago?"

"Yes, sir."

"You monitored it?"

"Yes, sir. If you'll wait just a second." Chambrun waited, drumming with the fingers of his left hand on the desk. Mrs. Kiley came back. "Outside phone, sir. Asked for seven twenty-two. We started the tape rolling. You care to hear it?"

"Please."

We could hear the tape start to run and then Coughlin's voice.

"Dr. Coughlin here."

A man's voice, strange to me. "Is Mr. Chambrun there?"

Coughlin: "Yes, he is."

Man: "Will you tell him that Miss Malone is waiting for him in his office?"

Coughlin: "Yes, I'll tell him."

Then came the click of a disconnect.

"That's it, sir," Mrs. Kiley said.

"And it was an outside call?"

"Yes, sir."

"Do you recognize the voice, Mrs. Kiley?"

"No, sir."

Chambrun switched off the squawk box and stood there, looking at us.

"Outside call means what?" Peter asked.

" 'Outside' means that it was not from one of the rooms or the house phones connected with the switchboard," I told him.

"Outside the hotel?"

"Not necessarily. There are dozens of pay phones in the lobby, the shops, the bars and restaurants. The call can have been made from any one of dozens of places inside the hotel. 'Outside' to Mrs. Kiley means a call she can't check through the switchboard."

"But why this false message to you, Mr. Chambrun?" Miss Ruysdale asked. "It doesn't make sense."

"The answer seems clear enough," Chambrun said. "We were wanted out of seven twenty-two, or off the seventh floor."

"Why?"

"Let's see if we can find out," Chambrun said.

CHAPTER 3

We went down to the lobby where we added Jerry Dodd to our party. On the way up to seven Chambrun filled him in.

"The girl's room is seven-o-seven," Jerry reminded us. "Same floor, different corridor."

"It was searched," Chambrun said. "Maggio had the housekeeper search it."

"That was an hour ago," Jerry said. "Maybe somebody wanted to get her back in her room and couldn't risk it while you were on the floor."

It was an idea, but it didn't check out. Laura's room was empty. The bed was neatly turned down, as it would have been by the floor maid early in the evening. In the closet were four street dresses, an evening gown, and an evening wrap. There was a faint scent of perfume that made her seem very real to me.

Her suitcase had been unpacked and rested on a rack to the right of the bureau. The bureau revealed handkerchiefs, some underthings. On the top of it, under the dressing mirror, were some jars; skin cream, makeup of some sort, an eyebrow pencil. There was a little spray thing of perfume, a comb and brush. She had come to stay, unpacked, arranged her things. There was no sign that she'd been back here since she'd joined us in the early evening and then begun patrolling the hotel.

Around the corner we rang the bell of 722. Dr. Coughlin answered. He looked surprised.

"Sorry to bother you again, Doctor," Chambrun said. "But that telephone message you got for me was a phony. There was no one waiting in my office for me."

"Oh?"

"This is Mr. Dodd, my security officer," Chambrun said, introducing Jerry.

The doctor nodded. "Come in. I don't know what I can do to help you, Mr. Chambrun—but come in."

The room was just as we'd left it twenty-odd minutes ago.

"You didn't by any chance recognize the voice on the telephone, did you, Doctor?" Chambrun asked.

"A man," Coughlin said. "Nothing familiar about him. I supposed he was one of your staff. He obviously knew you were here."

"There's only one possible reason for that fake call," Chambrun said. "Somebody wanted to get me out of this room or off this floor."

"Why?"

"One thought occurs to me," Chambrun said. "Someone

140

wanted to get to you or to your patient. Has anyone come here since we left? A maid, a waiter, a bellboy—anyone?"

"Not a soul."

"It's going on two o'clock in the morning, Doctor. Are you planning to spend the night with your patient?"

"As a matter of fact I was just about to leave," Coughlin said. "I gave Jim Gregory something to help him sleep a few minutes before you came here the first time. I've been waiting to make sure it worked. I just checked on him and he's sound asleep."

"Can we look in on him?"

"My dear man, Jim struggles to get rest," Coughlin said. "It would be cruel to wake him up. Why do you want to look in on him?"

Chambrun's eyes were cold as two newly minted dimes. "I'd like to make sure that he isn't Neil Drury."

The doctor's jaw dropped. Then he laughed. "You still think I might be Drury's cosmetician?"

"There's murder cooking, Doctor; violence. I'd be a fool if I didn't check out on the wildest possibilities."

Coughlin nodded, slowly. "I guess you would," he said. "What you'll see in the next room is the wreck of a man. He's suffering from terminal emphysema. I give him only a few months to live. He's dropped down from a hundred and ninety to about a hundred and forty pounds. You'll just have to look at him to know that he can't be your man. To start with, he's sixty-five years old; much older than your man."

"I'd like to see him," Chambrun said. "In a situation like this I don't take any man's word for what's behind a closed door."

"Jim Gregory is behind that door," Coughlin said. "I'd be deeply grateful if you'd try not to wake him."

He moved over to the bedroom door and opened it, carefully. The room beyond was partially dark. There was a small, shaded night-light on the table beside the bed. It wasn't part of standard equipment. It gave enough light to reveal the face of the man on the bed.

I had never seen James Gregory before, but I was shocked, as one is shocked by severe illness or death. The face was fish-belly white. The skin was drawn tight over high cheekbones. The closed eyes were sunk in deep sockets. His breathing was tortured. A sheet covered the body, but it didn't conceal the fact that Gregory was skin and bones.

On the table beside the light was an oxygen mask. It was evidently attached to a tank I couldn't see on the other side of the bed.

Chambrun stood staring at him for a moment or two and then he backed out of the room with the rest of us. Coughlin closed the door and faced us.

"Satisfied?" he asked. There was a touch of resentment in his voice.

"What is he doing here in the hotel?" Chambrun said. "He looks as if he could die before morning."

Coughlin took a cigarette out of his pocket and lit it. "There is so little you can do for a man in Jim's condition," he said. "You have a terminal cancer case and all you can do is give him enough drugs to make the agony less acute. In this case Jim will strangle to death because he can't get air. There is nothing I can do for him."

"So why bring him here?"

"Jim was a writer, a journalist. He's lived all around the world," Coughlin said. "He's well off, financially. His pleasure in life has been the fancy places: Paris, Rome, London, Athens, the Riviera, the best hotels, the best women. He has ups and downs in this sickness. A few days ago he was up. 'I don't want to sit here in your clinic, waiting to die,' he told me. 'I want to do the town once more.'" Coughlin shook his head. "There was no point in telling him that the moment he made the effort he would conk out. So I arranged for him to come here, where I could get to him in an emergency. As I foresaw, just the effort of getting here was too much for him. He hasn't been able to leave his room since he got here."

"Dr. Partridge is filled in on the medical facts of the case?" Chambrun asked.

"Perfectly," Coughlin said. "I dropped in tonight as a friend. Partridge is quite capable of handling any emergency."

"And that emergency could come any time?"

Coughlin shrugged. "Tomorrow, a month from tomorrow. Jim is a scrapper, bless him. He wants to spend one evening in the Blue Lagoon. We're going to do our best to let him have that final spree."

"I'm sorry to have gotten in your hair, Doctor."

"No problem."

"I'm concerned about that telephone call," Chambrun said. "It wasn't some kind of a malicious trick, a practical-joke kind of malice. There was a purpose behind it, and it can only have been to get me away from here—or at least from this area of the hotel. You may know from Partridge that Miss Malone is Drury's former girl friend. What you don't know is that she's disappeared and that we're hunting for her. That's why the message you gave me was bound to take me away from here on the run."

"I don't understand why," Coughlin said.

"Something else you don't know," Chambrun said, "is that Miss Malone has a room on this floor. It could be that it wasn't just to get me away from this suite but from this floor—this part of the hotel. There's no explanation of it in Miss Malone's room. There's no sign that she's been back there or that anyone has gone through her things. That brings us back to this suite, Doctor."

"Jigsaw puzzle with some missing pieces," Coughlin said.

"I find myself wondering if the missing pieces could be in that bedroom," Chambrun said, nodding toward Gregory's door.

Coughlin's face showed complete surprise. "Jim?" he said.

"I came up here for a special reason," Chambrun said. "I wanted to talk to Mr. Gregory and I wanted Mr. Williams to hear him in conversation. Of course, once I'd seen Mr. Gregory I wouldn't have needed Mr. Williams. But in the process of talking to Gregory I would probably have mentioned Drury and General Chang. He's been an around-the-world journalist. He might have heard something, remembered some detail, that would have been helpful. Do you suppose that's why they contrived to get me away from here?"

" 'They'?"

" 'They' are always the enemy," Chambrun said, with a faint smile. "If you're a Conservative, 'They' are the Liberals. If you're a Communist, 'They' are the capitalists. In this case 'They' might also be friends of Drury's who don't want us to get in his way. I think I'd like to talk to Mr. Gregory when he comes out of his drugged sleep—unless you have some serious objection, Doctor."

"None whatever," Coughlin said. "I'm sure it would interest him, and anything that interests him helps to make his last stretch of time a little more bearable."

"Again, thanks for everything, Doctor."

"Been a pleasure." Coughlin grinned. "For God sake, when you drop the other shoe, let me know. Otherwise I might die of curiosity."

Chambrun, I suspect, was keyed to a kind of total efficiency that morning at two o'clock. I was groggy, and could sense

Peter's fatigue from the way he hung onto my arm. Chambrun walked toward the elevators, brisk as a man who'd just gotten up from an eight-hour sleep. Peter and Jerry and I dragged after him. We'd all been at it for a straight sixteen hours.

It was a jigsaw puzzle all right, as far as I was concerned, with more missing pieces than I cared to think about. I suspect my trouble was that I wasn't really concerned with anything except what had happened to Laura. I had the feeling Peter was with me on that.

Suppose Drury had managed to get a message to her? Suppose she had gone outside the hotel to meet him? She probably wouldn't care a damn about my anxiety for her, but it seemed odd to me she wouldn't make some effort to get in touch with Peter. She must know how uptight he would be.

I said something to that effect as we walked along the second-floor corridor to Chambrun's office. Chambrun just looked at me and kept on walking. In the outer office we found Miss Ruysdale, looking as fresh as the boss, standing beside a table at which David Tolliver, Drury's agent, was seated. He had a stack of cards in front of him—registration cards. He needed a shave. He looked as if he'd been pulled out from under a rock somewhere. Miss Ruysdale introduced him to Chambrun and Jerry.

"Grateful to you for helping," Chambrun said.

"I wish I know what I was supposed to be doing," Tolliver said. He leaned back in his chair and rubbed his eyes with the knuckles of his hands. "There are hundreds of people in your hotel who would know the old Neil Drury by sight; casual acquaintances, maybe even a friend or two. But baskets full of movie fans, Mr. Chambrun. But we all know the old Neil Drury is gone; his face changed."

"I'm not looking for people who would recognize him as

he was," Chambrun said. "I'm looking for friends who might help him stay hidden; who might be cooperating with him in some way. If he came to you and asked you for help, Mr. Tolliver, would you help him?"

"You know it."

"Help him to commit a murder which will result in his getting killed himself?"

Tolliver lowered his hands. "I'd try to talk him out of it," he said. "That's why I put Mr. Haskell in touch with Peter. I thought if anyone could talk him out of it Peter could; and, of course, Laura Malone."

"That's why he's staying out of sight," Peter said. "He knows Laura and I might just convince him." He drew a deep breath. "I keep dreaming that's what Laura is doing right now."

"She could persuade him if anyone can," Tolliver said.

"So maybe they're riding around Central Park in a hansom cab, arguing about it," Chambrun said.

"But you don't believe that," Tolliver said.

"I wish I did," Chambrun said. "Does the name Sam Schwartz mean anything to you?"

"The first card I showed him," Miss Ruysdale said.

"Hollywood is full of guys who fit his description," Tolliver said. "Touts, pimps, tinhorn gamblers, gofors for the big shots."

"Gofors?"

"People who go for things for the big shots—glorified errand boys, message carriers," Tolliver said. "Some of them make a good living just by saying 'yes' and 'glad to get it for you.'"

"He's hooked into this," Chambrun said, "I suspect, with Chang. But he could be on the other side; a gofor for Drury. If you saw him would you know?"

Tolliver shrugged. "Might or might not," he said. "Neil wasn't the old-fashioned Hollywood big shot. He didn't have a crew of hangers-on. He didn't ever put on any side. He didn't have an army of behind-kissing friends."

"Someone phoned Schwartz when I was on my way up to see him and told him it had 'hit the fan.' That had to mean that someone knew he was on some list of mine. The warning could have come from someone on Chang's payroll, or it could have been Drury or some friend of his. Will you be willing to go with Jerry and take a look at Schwartz and see if he rings any bell with you?"

"Sure," Tolliver said.

Jerry Dodd grinned. "Brother Schwartz isn't going to be happy to be waked up again. You may really get yourself a lawsuit, boss."

"Help to occupy my spare time," Chambrun said, drily. He walked on into his own office. Peter and I dragged after him. He went straight to the Turkish coffee maker. Maybe that's what kept him so chipper. He turned to us, balancing the cup and saucer in the palm of his left hand.

"You evidently think I'm not concerning myself enough with the whereabouts of Laura Malone, Mark."

"I didn't say that."

"It's what's on your mind," he said. "There can be several reasons why she hasn't gotten in touch with Peter—or with you, my moonstruck friend. First and most obvious, she can't. She's been picked up by Chang's people with the idea of using her as a hostage if they don't find Drury in a hurry. Or Ruysdale's right, and she's had an accident of some sort we haven't been able to trace yet. Or she's with Drury and he doesn't want her to call you."

"Or she's dead," Peter said, in a flat voice.

"Or she's dead," Chambrun said, with the same emotion

he might have shown if he was discussing the price of eggs. "Second, she hasn't gotten in touch with you or Peter or anyone else because that's the way she wants it."

"Why should she want deliberately to scare the hell out of us?" I asked.

"There is one thing in this whole cockeyed story that I find it hard to buy," Chambrun said. "We've both heard it from Peter; you heard it from Laura. It's the love story, friends. It has a ring of truth to it. Those two people—the girl and Drury—met in a strange way and in the space of twenty-four hours became bound together in an almost classic involvement. So tragedy struck them. Drury's whole purpose in life was altered. Ring of truth. But then it goes off the tracks for me. He never got directly in touch again with the woman he loved. No letter. No phone call. He loved her so very much, and yet nothing."

"He was afraid Laura would talk him out of concentrating on Chang," Peter said.

"If he was so determined, no one could have talked him out of it," Chambrun said.

"If he continued his relationship with Laura, she'd have been in danger," I suggested. "Chang was looking for him. If she knew where he was, Chang might have forced her to talk."

"But not one last visit, no phone call, not even a letter? No explanation? No swearing of eternal vows?" Chambrun took a sip of his coffee. I had no sensible answer for him, nor did Peter, it seemed. "In my judgment, either the whole love story as we've heard it is a phony, or he has been in touch with her."

"So what does it matter which is true?" Peter asked. He had dropped down into one of the armchairs and covered his face with his hands.

"It matters a great deal," Chambrun said. "For me the love story rings true, as I've said, therefore the story that Drury has never been in touch with his woman—not once in five years—simply doesn't add up. So that brings us to another reason why you haven't heard from her. She's working with Drury. She's always known where he was. All that talk about 'sensing his presence' is hog wash. She knows where he is, she knows what he looks like, she's helping him. Nothing's happened to her that she didn't want to have happened. She slipped out of sight intentionally. She could expect there would be a total concentration on finding her."

"But *why?*" Peter asked.

"If we're concentrating on her, Drury will be freer to move around. It would be nice to find her, but I'm not sweating over her immediate safety. She's with Drury. You can count on it."

"Well, at least, then, she's safe," Peter said.

"Safe!" Chambrun snorted. "My dear, addlepated friend, no one close to Drury is safe. Just an innocent bystander in the line of fire between Chang and Drury is in danger. Chang is no fool. If he doesn't have Laura Malone as a hostage, then he's come to the same conclusion I have. She's with Drury. Finding Drury is difficult. None of us can identify him by sight. But now Chang knows that if he can find Laura, whom he can identify, he will be very close to Drury. Safe?" His coffee cup rattled as he put it down on his desk. "There is a thorough and methodical search of the hotel going on. Our people and Wexler's people are on the lookout for her. Unless either of you has a brain storm—?" He looked at us with his bright black eyes narrowed. "You, Peter—you and Tolliver are the good friends of Drury's I know about. Who else in New York? Who could Drury go to, persuade to help him? Laura can be hidden away in somebody's apartment, blocks from here. That apartment can be Drury's headquarters and not the Beaumont. Surely you can come up with a list of people?"

Peter shook his head. "Neil didn't have many close friends," he said. "It started when we were adolescents. I don't know of any one else from that period he kept in touch with. He had hundreds of warm acquaintances, you might say—people who liked him, admired him, laughed with him. But not close. Even Tolliver isn't close in a personal way. He and Neil had a first-class business arrangement, but it wasn't an intimacy. I was in his confidence, and of course Laura. If there is anyone else as close as we were, I have no way of knowing about it."

Chambrun took a deep drag on his Egyptian cigarette and let the smoke out in a long sigh. "So much for the frank and open Mr. Drury." He put out his cigarette with a sort of angry twisting gesture in the ashtray. "I suggest to you two that you try to get a few hours' sleep. Drury isn't going to get to General Chang tonight. There's simply no way to break through that twelfth-floor security. But tomorrow, when Chang decides to visit the United Nations; when he insists on looking over the Grand Ballroom for his bloody birthday party—that's when we can anticipate action. It would be helpful if you were both in something better than a comatose condition."

"Sleep isn't going to come easy," Peter said.

"Then take something!"

I was just pulling myself up, wearily, out of my chair when Miss Ruysdale came in from the outer office.

"The Madwoman of Chaillot," she said.

Chambrun looked startled. "Here?" He glanced at his watch.

"On the phone," Miss Ruysdale said. She was fighting a

smile. "You are to present yourself immediately at Penthouse L."

"At two-thirty in the morning?"

"The foyer outside her apartment is crowded with policemen," Miss Ruysdale said. "The roof outside her house is crowded with policemen. Her privacy is destroyed. Unless this situation is remedied immediately she will put in a phone call to Mr. Battles in France and have your scalp."

"Oh, God," Chambrun said. "Hardy has men up there so that the roof doesn't get tramped on before they have a chance in daylight to finish examining it. Since Li Sung and his killer found their way up there he has a man watching for some kind of repeat performance."

"You must remove them," Miss Ruysdale said, the smile getting a little better of her.

"Go up and try to explain it to her, Ruysdale," Chambrun said.

"I am in Mrs. Haven's black book," Miss Ruysdale said. The Madwoman of Chaillot was Mrs. George Haven. She had lived in the Penthouse, a cooperatively owned unit, since the hotel was built. She predated Chambrun. She appeared, imperiously, in the lobby from time to time, wearing an early 1900 hat that looked like a fruit bowl, an ancient mink coat that fitted her like a tent, with a little Japanese spaniel, a mean, sneering little beast, tucked under her arm.

"I once neglected to say good morning to Toto," Miss Ruysdale said. "He had bitten my finger the last time I spoke to him." She looked at me. "The old gal is much more likely to be conned by a young and attractive male. I suggest Mark would be ideal."

"Go talk to the old girl and explain we're trying to protect her, Mark," Chambrun said. "Two-thirty in the morning!"

I took Peter down the hall to my place. I had some seconal

tablets in my bathroom and I gave him a couple to help him sleep. Then I headed for the upper reaches.

At almost any other time I would have been glad of the chance to get into Penthouse L. I had heard rumors about its extraordinary disarray. Tonight I was dead on my feet.

The elevator opened right into the outside foyer of Penthouse L. As I stepped out I found myself facing one of Hardy's men whom I knew from the past, a detective named Penzner. He grinned at me.

"A diplomatic messenger?" he asked. He took his hand off the butt of the gun he was wearing in a holster.

"Never send a boy to do a man's work, I always say," I said. "But the boss is busy."

"The old lady is a volcano about to erupt," Penzner said. "She won't listen to my explanations. Good luck."

I rang the doorbell, and the door was instantly opened by Mrs. Haven herself, wearing an incredible lace-bedecked housecoat that looked like something children had gotten together for a masquerade. Her mouth was open, ready to deliver a blast at Chambrun. Instead, she spoke in a reasonable tone for her.

"Oh, it's you, Haskell. Come in." She had the booming voice of a nineteenth-century character actress playing the Queen Mother in Hamlet. She didn't wait for me. She just set sail for the interior.

I had never seen anything like the room I found myself in. It looked like a glorified junk shop. There was twice as much furniture as it could properly hold, most of it Victorian. Heavy red velvet curtains blotted out the windows. Bookcases overflowed into stacks and piles of volumes on the floor. Sunday papers from the last six months were scattered about. The disorder was colossal, and yet I noticed there wasn't a speck of dust in the place. What was disorder to me was obviously order to Mrs. Haven. I had a feeling that if I asked for it she could probably put her fingers on the editorial page from the *Times* of last winter.

"Will you have some tea, Haskell?"

"No, thank you, ma'am. I just came up because—"

"I insist," she said. She sailed out and left me alone—I thought.

I looked around, aware that the place was stiflingly hot, and that there was the sweet, sickening odor of some kind of incense burning. The walls, I saw, were a solid mass of photographs, most of them personally autographed to "Constance Haven" with affectionate salutes. The old lady had really known some people in her day. There were three presidents—Teddy Roosevelt, Woodrow Wilson, and Warren G. Harding. There was an enormous blown-up portrait of Theda Bara, the old silent-movie vamp. There were famous actors and actresses, writers, painters, figures in high society of another time. There was a picture of a quite beautiful and young Mrs. Haven riding on the box of a coach and four, driven by an elegant gentleman in a gray topper. The writing had faded, but the driver was evidently an early Vanderbilt.

I moved around, looking for faces I knew. I came on one without an inscription. It was a young, solid-looking man, with a pleasant, smiling face. I was certain I'd seen him some place before, but I couldn't recall who he was or where I'd seen him. I was trying to dredge it up when Mrs. Haven trumpeted at me.

"Your tea, Haskell."

The tea was in a delicate little china cup. It tasted perfumed. I sat down in a chair I was sure would collapse but it didn't. I waved at the pictures.

"You've had a very rich life in terms of friends, Mrs.

Haven," I said.

"Now tell me what all this police nonsense is about," she said, ignoring my comment.

She knew about the murder of Li Sung, of course. She'd been questioned by Hardy, and Wexler, and Larch, and God knows who else.

"We don't know what the dead man was doing on the roof, Mrs. Haven," I said, trying to sip the tea without making a face. "You are aware that there's a threat of violence in the hotel surrounding General Chang."

"If a man lives by violence, he can expect to die violently," Mrs. Haven said, as if she was quoting from some childhood maxim.

"We want to prevent it," I said. "As for the men on the roof, the police didn't get here until after dark. They don't want the place messed up until they can give it a thorough examination by daylight."

"And that idiot outside my front door?"

"They don't want anyone getting to you, Mrs. Haven, who shouldn't. They don't want anyone getting out on the roof from the foyer."

"I sent a message to Chambrun," she said, "but he was evidently too pigeon-livered to come up here himself. I don't blame you, Haskell, but Chambrun is going to hear from the powers that be. When I ask him for something, I expect the courtesy of personal attention."

"He sent his abject apology to you, Mrs. Haven," I said. So I was a diplomat. "He is involved with the efforts to prevent a violence. And he has no authority to order these policemen away from the roof, or from outside your door."

"Those miserable creatures on the roof are probably waiting for a chance to peep at me when I disrobe for the night!"

I thought that back in the days when she'd ridden on a

coach and four with a Vanderbilt she would probably have been right.

"There have been quite a few Peeping Toms in my life," she said.

"I can well believe that, Mrs. Haven," I said.

She smiled at me and I guessed that before her face had withered the smile had been pretty devastating. "It's nice to know that chivalry is not entirely dead, Haskell." She stood up. I was about to be dismissed. "Since nothing can be done about the men, I suppose I am helpless. Nonetheless, I want to talk to Chambrun as early as possible in the morning—if he can disengage himself from that fancy secretary of his. I will not have these men camping out here forever. I used to know the Mayor when he was a small boy and I will get him here tomorrow to put an end to this if I have to."

"I'll tell Mr. Chambrun," I said.

I started for the door.

"I see you didn't enjoy the tea, Haskell. You should have asked for whiskey."

I was sorry, in a way, to leave her. I imagined she would be a fascinating person to talk to about the past when she wasn't worried about Peeping Toms. Maybe part of the trouble was she knew she had no reason to worry any more.

I was too tired to get any further than my room. I tiptoed through to the bedroom, not wanting to wake Peter, who was sound asleep on the bed-sofa. Evidently the seconal had worked. I called Miss Ruysdale on my bedside phone and told her Mrs. Haven would at least hold her fire till morning.

"She wants to see Chambrun then," I said, "if—and I quote—'he can disengage himself from that fancy secretary of his.'"

"Dirty old woman," Miss Ruysdale said. "Incidentally, if

you care, there is no news."

"Goodnight, Ruysdale."

I undressed and crawled, naked, under a sheet. I turned off the bed lamp, and it could only have been seconds before I went to sleep. It wasn't a restful sleep. It was full of dreams—dreams about Laura in the nightmare clutches of a grinning Chang; dreams of a young Constance Haven without any clothes on, surrounded by an army of leering men. Suddenly I was sitting bolt upright in bed, wide-awake.

I knew who the man was in the picture that had bothered me. I had seen another picture of him when he was older than the version on Mrs. Haven's wall.

He was Walter Drury, Neil Drury's father.

CHAPTER 4

I'd seen the senior Drury's picture in the clippings Tolliver had in his office. I guessed the one on Mrs. Haven's wall had been taken twenty years earlier than the clipping, which dated back only some five years to the time of the Drury family's arrival in Buenos Aires. But the pose was the same, the smile the same. Have you noticed how often men in public life will adopt the same pose when they're confronted by photographers?

I scrambled out of bed, very wide-awake now, and got into some clothes. I was tempted to wake Peter, but he was so deep in sleep that he didn't even stir as I flurried about.

Down the hall in Chambrun's outer office Miss Ruysdale was just putting the cover on her typewriter. Three-thirty in the morning is a late quitting time, and I thought I saw the nearest thing to a slightly hostile look in her eyes as I barged in.

"You said you'd prepared a set of clippings for me on the Drury business," I said. "I never saw them because I'd already seen Tolliver's set and I had Peter in tow."

"I have them here," Miss Ruysdale said. She handed me a manila folder from the wire basket on her desk. There it was, right on the top—a duplicate of the picture I'd seen in Tolliver's office. It showed Drury, his wife and daughter, on their arrival in South America.

My finger shook a little as I pointed to the ambassador's picture. "There's a photograph of this man hanging on the wall of Mrs. Haven's living room." I swallowed hard. "It was taken a number of years before this one, but it's the same guy." I told her how I'd seen it, hadn't been able to place it, and waked up out of a sound sleep with the answer ready.

"Mr. Chambrun promised he'd catch himself a nap, but I guess I'd better call him," she said.

There's a small room opening off Chambrun's office where he has a cot which he rarely uses. He was lying there on his back, but with his eyes open when Miss Ruysdale and I went in. He listened, then sat up and tightened his tie, took his coat off the back of a chair and put it on.

"Let's you and I go have a look at it," he said.

"Shall I tell her you're coming?" Ruysdale asked. "She's probably bedded down by now."

"The odds are about eight to five that she's expecting us," Chambrun said.

"How come?"

"She saw you looking at the photograph, didn't she, Mark?"

We took the long trip to the roof in an elevator now on

self-service. Detective Penzner looked surprised to see us.

"Anyone come or go since Haskell was here a while ago?" Chambrun asked.

"One of the boys on the roof went down to get some coffee. Came back," Penzner said.

"No one for Mrs. Haven?"

"No, sir."

Chambrun rang the doorbell. Mrs. Haven couldn't have been in bed. She was still wearing that absurd housecoat as she opened the door.

"Well, Pierre," she said, "you do choose the oddest times."

"I'm sorry, Constance," he said.

I stared at them. The exchange of first names was a complete surprise and told a story I hadn't dreamed of. All her screaming at and about him, all his shuddering at the prospect of having to see her, was a fraud. These two, at a rock-bottom level I hadn't seen before, had a relationship that was at least on the warm side.

"Haskell conveyed your apology," Mrs. Haven said. "It wasn't necessary for you to come tonight."

"I think you know I haven't come to apologize," Chambrun said.

"For whatever reason, come in," she said. "Both of you."

We walked into the living room. There was only one change. My tea cup had gone from the coffee table and a bottle of bonded bourbon had taken its place. There was a half-empty shot glass beside it.

"You will help me ease my conscience," Mrs. Haven said. "I don't normally drink alone. You care for ice, gentlemen, or will you take it neat?"

"Neat will be fine," Chambrun said.

The old lady swept out of the room. I went over to the wall and pointed to Walter Drury's photograph. Mrs. Haven came back with two glasses while we were looking at it.

"If I had been young enough, I'd have twisted that young man around my little finger," she said.

"You know who he is?"

She laughed. "I don't have pictures of strangers on my wall, Pierre. Of course I know who he is. Walter Drury."

"I meant do you know who he is in relation to what's been going on in this hotel for the last day and a half?" Chambrun said.

"Of course I do. He was the father of a man you're looking for, Neil Drury."

"Well, at least we don't have to play the game of tomato surprise," Chambrun said. He didn't seem to be in a hurry. I guess he knew his woman. She poured us each a three-ounce slug of bourbon, refilled her own glass, and sat down.

"Well, get on with it, Pierre," she said.

"How well do you know Neil Drury," Chambrun said.

"Not well at all," Mrs. Haven said. "When he was a very small boy—three, four years old—I visited the Drurys for a week at their place in the Berkshires. He was like any little boy; in and out; not in one's hair, if you know what I mean; nice mannered."

"That would be more than thirty years ago, Constance. How well did you get to know him between then and now?"

"Not at all, really," the old lady said. "At a debutante party when he was in college. I was not coming out, you understand. I was a chaperone. Some years later I was invited to an open house at The Players—actors' club, you know. It was founded by Edwin Booth back in—"

"I know about The Players, Constance," Chambrun said, pressing just a little.

"Well, I met Neil there, quite by accident, on that open-house evening. We reminded each other that we knew each other. I inquired into the state of health of his parents, particularly my dear old friend Walter, and that was that."

"And the next time you saw him?

"I don't think I have ever seen him since that night."

"You 'don't think'?"

She took a generous swallow of her whiskey neat. "My dear Pierre, let us not quibble. I read the papers. I hear a great deal of gossip from your blabber-mouthed staff. If you knew the dirt I get on people from the maids and the housekeeper, you'd be shocked. I know that Neil has had his face changed by some sort of operation. So I can only say what is true, Pierre. I 'don't think' I have seen him since that night some years ago at The Players. If he's in the hotel, if he's been here for the last few days or weeks, I haven't been aware of it. But of course, with a changed face, how can I be certain. Therefore I tell you I 'don't think' I've seen him."

"You're telling me that he's not been in touch with you, Constance?"

"You didn't ask me if he'd been in touch with me."

"My dear Constance, I am a very tired man. I am a man enmeshed in very severe tensions. I am trying to prevent a man or men from being murdered. I don't want to play parlor games with you, or be forced to make certain that the questions I ask you are phrased exactly to your liking. May I start over?"

"Be my guest, Pierre," the old lady said. She made it sound light, but her faded blue eyes looked deeply troubled. She sipped her whiskey and then dabbed at her rouged lips with a lace-edged handkerchief.

Chambrun looked very directly at her. "Is Neil Drury here in your apartment, Constance?"

"Of course not," she said, promptly. "I told you that to my knowledge I haven't seen him for some years. And there are no strange men hiding away here either, Pierre, more's the pity." She tried to make it sound gay.

"Fine. I believe you," Chambrun said. "But forgive me if I stop beating around the bush. Is Laura Malone here?"

The old lady put her empty shot glass down hard on the table. "Damn you, Pierre!" she said.

"Will you tell her it's very necessary for me to talk to her now, at once," Chambrun said.

"Before I do, Pierre, may I ask you a question or two?"

I was on my feet. Laura was here!

Chambrun sighed. "Quick questions, Constance."

"Is there any legal reason why Laura shouldn't be here in my apartment?" Mrs. Haven asked.

"None that I know of," Chambrun said in a tired voice.

"Is she wanted by the police? Is there a warrant out for her?"

"No."

"She is in no way connected with the murder that took place on my roof. She was actually with Wexler's man, on her way here, when it happened."

"I believe she was."

"Then what do you want to see her for?"

"I believe you and she are helping Neil Drury to get himself killed," Chambrun said. "And if you are helping him you are helping to plan the assassination of General Chang, which is a criminal offense, whether Neil Drury pulls it off or not."

"Thanks for trying, Mrs. Haven," Laura's voice said from behind me.

I spun around and saw her standing in the doorway. She stood very straight, her head high. I saw that her hands were clenched in two fists at her side.

"I'm sorry, my dear," Mrs. Haven said. "I cannot lie to Pierre. I can evade him, but I cannot lie to him."

"I understand, Mrs. Haven," Laura said in that low, husky voice.

"Do you know what you've put us through?" I said, my anger showing.

"Do be quiet, Haskell," Mrs. Haven said. I heard the clink of the whiskey bottle against the rim of her glass.

Chambrun's face had that rock-hard look to it I knew so well. "Where is Neil Drury?" he asked, dangerously quiet.

"I'm sorry," Laura said.

He turned his head slightly. "Where is he, Constance?"

"I don't have the faintest idea, Pierre. I have asked not to be told anything I couldn't repeat to you."

"But you know that he's close by somewhere and that he's planning to kill a man?"

"Everybody knows that, Pierre," Mrs. Haven said. "You know it, the government knows it, General Chang knows it, even the newspapers know it. Is there something sinister about my knowing it?"

"But you have been hiding Miss Malone."

"I don't believe 'hiding' is quite the proper word for it, Pierre," Mrs. Haven said "Laura is a friend of Neil Drury's. I am a friend of his, and was a close friend of his family's. She asked if she might spend some time here. I told her she could. Period."

"You're aware, Miss Malone, that dozens of men have been searching this hotel from top to bottom, looking for you?" Chambrun asked. "That there is a general alarm for you and the city police are combing the area outside the hotel? That you have driven Mark and your friend Peter Williams into a state of dithering anxiety?"

"I'm sorry."

"You choose not to talk?"

"I'm sorry." It was a broken record, a kind of zombie

162

response.

Chambrun stared at her for a moment and then walked over to the telephone. He was promptly connected with the switchboard. "Chambrun here," he said. "Locate Jerry Dodd and ask him to come up to Penthouse L on the double." He put down the receiver. "I'm not sure, Miss Malone, that it makes much difference whether you talk or not. Nothing you have told us from the beginning has been true. You've clearly been in touch with Drury all along. The sad story of his dropping out of your life is an untruth. Whatever his plan is to get at General Chang, you're part of it. You didn't have to sense his presence. You've always known where he is and how to reach him. You could tell us what he looks like. You could tell us how many other people are involved in the plot. The one thing that puzzles me is why you've chosen to blow your cover by disappearing. Of course it didn't blow your cover until we found you, did it? You were still the helpless, lovable girl in the hands of General Chang's killers till we found you." His eyes flicked to Mrs. Haven who was putting quite a dent in the bourbon without any outward effect. "It was careless of you to leave Walter Drury's picture on the wall, Constance."

She laughed, like a little girl playing a parlor game. "Would you believe I'd forgotten it was there, Pierre?" She waved at the portrait gallery. "All old friends. I had actually forgotten Walter Drury's face was among them."

Chambrun looked at her steadily for a moment and then turned back to Laura. "You might as well find yourself a chair, Miss Malone," he said. "You're not going anywhere."

"You have a right to stop her from leaving, Pierre?"

"I've gone quite a way past caring what my rights are, Constance," he said. He watched Laura move to a chair and lower herself into it. I had the feeling that her legs had become pretty weak under her.

"Constance, how much do you know about the murder of Li Sung?" Chambrun asked.

"Nothing. Nothing whatever, Pierre. It's hard to believe, I know, because I was here in my apartment and Toto didn't give any sort of alarm. But that's how it was. What I've told the police is the exact truth."

"When did Miss Malone get in touch with you and ask to come up here?"

"A little before midnight. She came right up after that."

"How did she get by the man posted in the foyer?"

Mrs. Haven gave us that little girl giggle. "I told Laura there was a policeman there. She wanted to avoid him. So I invited him in for a cup of coffee and a sandwich. He was here to protect me, so as long as he was with me, in the kitchen—" She spread her bony hands, heavy with rings. "Laura just slipped in and waited for him to go. Rather clever, don't you think?"

"You'd waited all evening for the chance to give us the slip," Chambrun said to Laura. "Am I right in thinking that the purpose was to get us looking for you instead of Drury?"

She had lowered her head. She didn't answer.

"Had Drury told you to expect a call from Miss Malone, Constance?"

"I told you, Pierre, I haven't seen or been in touch with Neil."

"Do you know a man named Schwartz?"

"The toy manufacturer?"

"No, Constance, not the toy manufacturer. Do you know anyone named James Gregory?"

I thought she hesitated for just a second before she gave Chambrun another 'No.'

He turned back to Laura. "How good a chance do you think Drury's plan has?" he asked.

No answer.

"I don't suppose there's any point in making any sort of plea to you," Chambrun said. I sensed his rising anger. "Whatever Drury's scheme is, it's going to fail. There are too many people on both sides who are too well prepared, too efficient. He's persuaded you, obviously, that it will work. If it did—if he managed to get at Chang, which I doubt— he will never get away with it. He'll be killed on the spot, or he'll be taken alive by our people and spend the rest of his life in some joy-resort, like Attica. If they find that you have collaborated with him you will face the same kind of punishment. What the hell are you involved in, Miss Malone, a suicide pact? It's idiocy!"

She spoke for the first time. "I do what Neil asks me to do," she said.

"Then arrange for me to talk to him!" Chambrun said, sharply. "I'll go anywhere you say. I'll talk to him on a phone that can't be monitored. Let me tell him exactly how impregnable Chang's defenses are."

"He knows," she said.

"And still you're prepared to help get him killed?"

"Oh, come, Pierre, have you never been in love?" Mrs. Haven asked, jolly as all hell. "A woman who really loves a man may try to persuade him not to run risks, but if he insists she will go along with him."

The doorbell rang.

Chambrun nodded to me to answer it and I let Jerry Dodd in.

"What's cooking?" he asked. Then as he followed me into the room I heard him mutter under his breath: "Holy cow!" I don't think he'd seen Laura. His comment was on the junk shop. Then, when he did see Laura: "Well, this is a relief."

"I hope you continue to think so," Chambrun said. He gave Jerry a quick sketch of the situation. Jerry's bright little eyes were filled with disbelief.

"You must be off your rocker, Miss Malone," he said.

She didn't look at him.

"So now we're going to play this my way," Chambrun said. "I want the two best men you have up here, Jerry, inside the apartment."

"Right."

"I don't want you, or them, or anyone else to even whisper that we've found Miss Malone."

Jerry's eyebrows rose. "You'll have to tell Wexler and the cops."

"I don't have to tell anyone," Chambrun said. "Somebody's looking over Wexler's shoulder for Chang. I want Chang to think that we're still looking for Miss Malone. I want the search to go on. I don't want anyone to know it's a phony. I don't want anyone's foot to slip because they've relaxed, knowing it isn't for real."

"Right."

Chambrun walked over to the phone and talked to Mrs. Kiley. "No phone calls in or out of Penthouse L," he ordered, "unless it's Jerry Dodd or me. Absolutely no calls."

He put down the phone. Mrs. Haven was giving him a wide Cheshire cat smile. He turned and walked into the bedroom area. An asthmatic growl came from under a table loaded with Staffordshire dogs. Toto had been there all this time, luxuriating on a bright scarlet satin cushion without letting us know he'd been eavesdropping. He snuffled his pug nose and went back to sleep. Chambrun came back, carrying a telephone instrument in his hand. The wires had been pulled out from the wall.

"I remembered that you have a private outside line, Constance," he said.

CHAPTER 5

I told myself Mrs. Haven must be right; a woman in love will go along with her man no matter how wrong she may think he is. But Chambrun had laid it on the line to Laura without any ifs, ands, or buts. There wasn't any way Neil Drury could come out of this with a future. He would either be dead or shut away. And Laura had the same kind of prospects. There had to be some way to get to Drury and talk sense to him. Then I wondered if my mother and sister had been raped and murdered, and my father mowed down by gunfire, anything but revenge would make sense. You couldn't approach anything like normal in that kind of climate.

But we had to try, I told myself. We had to find Drury and try.

"If the girl couldn't sell him on the futility of what he's planning, we can't hope to have much chance," Chambrun said.

We were back in his office and Miss Ruysdale had been let in on the secret.

"Your old lady friend turned out to be something!" I said. I'd poured myself a drink, but it tasted lousy.

Chambrun gave me a faint smile. "Constance? A very special old biddy," he said. "I wonder if you know how special, Mark?"

"Who would have dreamed you were on a first-name basis with her," I said. I looked at Miss Ruysdale, expecting her to agree. Evidently it was no surprise to her.

Chambrun leaned back in his desk chair, his heavy eyelids lowered. "Thirty years ago Constance Haven was an expatriate living in Paris," he said. "The Nazi's held the city at the time. Those were the black days."

"You mean she's eighty years old?" I said, surprised. God knows there was nothing feeble about her.

"Eighty, eighty-one," Chambrun said. "I was twenty when I first met her, fighting in the French underground: the Resistance. Constance presided over a salon, all the big shots —the Germans and the collaborators. Patriotic Frenchmen viewed her with contempt and loathing, except those of us in the Resistance. She was one of our best sources of information."

"Well, I'll be damned," I said.

"A strange code of ethics," Chambrun said. "She tells the truth, but she has a way of playing games with it. But with me—well, we understand each other. Why do you suppose she sent for me in the middle of the night?"

"She wanted to get rid of the cops so that Laura and Drury could come and go at will," I said.

"I think not," Chambrun said. "She wanted me to see that photograph of Walter Drury."

"It was the wildest chance that I saw it," I said.

Chambrun's smile was almost affectionate. "If you hadn't stumbled on it, I think she'd have found a way to make sure that you did. You see, her loyalties were split. She's a sentimental slob and she'd been conned into helping the star-crossed lovers. She's also a hard-boiled realist, and she knew what they were walking into. She'd probably tried to talk Laura out of it—depend on it she hasn't seen Drury or she'd have admitted it to me. When that didn't work she turned to me, a friend. She had to do it in her own elliptical way. She couldn't seem to betray them because I think she still hopes to talk them out of it." He laughed. "Did you see that little-girl, I-just-swallowed-the-canary smile she gave me when I gave the orders to the switchboard that there were to be no calls in or out? She was reminding me that she had a private outside line. Constance is quite something."

"You can count on her to help, then."

"I can count on her to help. I can also count on her not telling me anything that she learns in confidence from Laura or Drury."

"Anyway they're safe up there. Cops and Jerry."

Chambrun's smile faded. "I wish I could be certain," he said. "You went up there; then I went up there; then Jerry Dodd. Chang's 'eyes' must know that. They must be guessing that there is something of special interest about Penthouse L. Li Sung died there."

"What about Peter?" I asked. "It seems rough not to let him know that Laura's turned up."

"By all means tell him," Chambrun said. "We need him to concentrate on finding Drury."

The first dawn light was showing through the windows of my bedroom when I flopped down on the bed again, without bothering to take off my clothes. Peter was so sound asleep in the living room that I thought it would be merciful to let him get all he could. There would be no one circulating in the Beaumont now except the house-cleaning crew that would be swabbing down the public rooms for another day.

My phone woke me. I glanced at my wrist watch as I reached for it. Nine thirty! I'd had almost five hours sleep and I should have been on the job long ago.

It was Miss Ruysdale on the phone. "I've let you have as much as I can, Mark. Mr. Chambrun will want you and Mr. Williams here in about fifteen minutes. You've just got time to shave, shower and dress. There'll be your kind of coffee here."

"All quiet on the roof?" I asked.

"All quiet."

My mouth felt like the inside of a birdcage. I went out into the living room and found Peter already up and dressed.

"I managed to make myself some instant coffee," he said. "Like some?"

"Come in the bathroom while I shave," I said. "I have some good news for you. We found Laura."

"Safe?"

"I also have some bad news for you. She's been flim-flamming us from the start." I gave him the whole story while I was lathering up.

"The fools," he said. "Don't they know they can't win? It's hard to believe Neil would let her run that kind of risk."

"Our problem is to find Drury and talk him out of it," I said. "Laura's tried, apparently, and failed. Now she'll do whatever he wants her to do."

"Maybe she'd listen to me," Peter said. His mouth twitched. "God knows I have reason enough to wish Chang dead; I understand better than anyone how Neil feels."

"Try it on Chambrun. We're meeting him in ten minutes."

The Great Man was at his desk when Peter and I walked into his office. So help me, he didn't look any different than he did any other morning. God knows how much sleep he'd managed.

"Peter thinks if he talked to Laura—" I began.

"Sit down," Chambrun said. "It needs thinking out."

Peter, his blackthorn stick hooked over his arm, walked to one of the leather armchairs and sat down. I perched on the arm of the other one.

"In about an hour," Chambrun said, "things will begin to get sticky. Chang is about to come out from behind his wall of protection, the twelfth floor. He is going to the United Nations for a conference with some of the delegates. On his way out of the hotel he plans to visit the Grand Ballroom to see if it will do for his birthday party, and to discuss details with me and Mr. Amato, the banquet manager. In other words, he is coming out into the open. He'll be surrounded by his own men, and by Larch's men, and by Wexler's people—and by ours. He'll be as safe as a man can be except in an hermetically sealed room. And yet, in spite of all the best planning, there are little chinks of daylight somewhere, almost certainly, that could be penetrated."

"You think Drury will try to act at once—not wait for a better opportunity?" I asked.

"He can't wait," Chambrun said. "We're getting too close to him. He has to be sweating over the possibility that Laura may change her mind and turn him in. Not a treachery, you understand, but he must be concerned that we may be able to persuade Laura that, if she loves him, she must help us prevent him from walking into certain death."

"I still dream I might persuade her," Peter said.

"Tolliver looked at Schwartz. No result, never saw him before," Chambrun said. "I've spent fifteen minutes this morning talking to James Gregory, the sick man in seven twenty-two. Since I haven't been able to guess why we were hoaxed away from that suite last night, I still thought it might have been to prevent me from talking to Gregory, that there might be something he knew that would help us."

"And was there?" I asked.

Chambrun shook his head. "It is, happily, one of Mr. Gregory's better days. He was sitting up in a chair having his breakfast. He still hopes to have 'a night on the town,' as he puts it. It's rather difficult to talk to a man who knows he's going to die. It—it gets in the way. But Gregory is a charming, cultivated, very sophisticated man. He has no illusions about his illness. He's in a race with the business of dying. All he wants is one gay evening. We did talk about Drury, however. Gregory knew the story, of course, as anyone does who was reading newspapers five years ago or listening to news broadcasts. He never met any of the Drurys, he told me. He sympathized with Neil Drury, sympathizes with him now. His career as a journalist has not made him a lover of the power boys of this world, like Chang. But he had nothing helpful to offer; has no idea why we might have been called away last night."

"Dead end," Peter muttered.

"We have almost no time left in which to find Drury," Chambrun said, "and either talk him out of his plan or sit on his head so that he can't carry through."

"Without Laura's help you'll never spot him," I said.

Chambrun nodded, slowly. He picked up the phone and pressed the button on the squawk box so we could hear his conversation. The switchboard answered. It was Mrs. Veach, the day supervisor.

"Yes, Mr. Chambrun?"

"Connect me with Jerry Dodd in Penthouse L, please." We could hear the ring sound and after a moment Jerry answered. "Chambrun here, Jerry. I want you to bring Miss Malone down to my office."

"If she'll come," Jerry said.

"Tell her we've found Drury," Chambrun said, blandly.

"No kidding!"

"Tell her that," Chambrun said.

"Oh, I get it. And suppose that doesn't work?"

"Drag her down here by the hair of her head," Chambrun said.

"That could make trouble, boss."

"I'll face the trouble," Chambrun said. He hung up the phone.

"She knows you haven't got Drury because she obviously knows where he is," Peter said.

"Yes, I think she knows," Chambrun said. He looked at me, his eyes hardly visible between narrowed slits. "You notice anything different about this office this morning, Mark?"

"Different?" I looked around. There wasn't anything I could see.

"A rearrangement of the furniture," Chambrun said.

"Oh, yes, I noticed you'd placed the chairs differently," I said.

Chambrun's voice was harsh. "So did Mr. Williams," he said.

Peter turned his head, the black goggles glittering in the sunlight that streamed through the windows.

"Mr. Williams' extraordinary talent for learning the geography of a room has impressed us both, Mark. But I find myself fascinated by his ability to walk directly to that chair where he's sitting when it isn't in the place where he's learned to expect it to be. No fumbling with his cane, no walking to the right place which this morning is the wrong place."

Peter sat up very straight in his chair, gripping the heavy blackthorn stick. "I don't know what you're talking about," he said.

"You can see," Chambrun said. "You made another slip

last night that started me wondering."

"What are you talking about—slip?"

"When we visited Robert Zabielski's room, the fellow who had the call girl with him, you made a slip. When we left I asked you about him. You were there to listen to his voice, remember? You said, 'Not possibly Neil. Wrong height, wrong size, wrong voice.' How could you know he was the wrong height and the wrong size unless you can see?"

"You described him to me before we went there," Peter said.

"Take off those goggles," Chambrun said. "We can stand what there is to see there."

I could feel the hair rising on the back of my neck.

Peter sat very still, gripping the blackthorn. "So I can see a little," he said, "but what's behind these glasses isn't pretty."

"A new medical miracle?" Chambrun asked. "Eyes that are gouged out replaced by a new set of eyes?" He turned in his chair and reached for a cigarette in the silver box on his desk. "A good many blind people have crossed my path in this business. Some of them are marvelously skillful at compensating for their disaster. But I've never seen anyone as good at it as you appeared to be. Tell me, where is the real Peter Williams? Where is the man whose eyes were really gouged out, Mr. Drury?"

I felt as though I'd been hit in the gut by a pile driver. I simply didn't believe it; Chambrun had to be wrong.

Slowly Peter raised his hands and took off the black goggles. The eyes behind them were narrowed slightly against the sudden bright light, but they were flawless, a cold gray blue. "I could have sworn I had you all fooled a hundred percent," he said.

"You are Neil Drury?" I asked. It was a vocal croak.

"Yes, Mark. I'm sorry to have had to take you in." He turned to Chambrun. "If you'll ask Miss Ruysdale to come in I'll make a statement for you."

Chambrun pressed the button on his desk. "It's for the best, Drury," Chambrun said. "You couldn't win, you know. You've got a life to live, you've got a woman who loves you —a very special woman."

A nerve twitched in Peter's—Drury's—cheek. "Sitting there in your chair, Chambrun, you can never know what this means to me. You can't even imagine what I feel, what I must have."

Miss Ruysdale appeared with her notebook. She looked at Drury without emotion. "So you were right," she said to Chambrun. She must have been in on moving the furniture; known the trap Chambrun was setting. Drury waved to the chair where he'd been sitting. She took it and sat there, waiting, her pencil poised over her notebook. Drury stood behind her.

"This is my statement," he said. Then something happened. The blackthorn stick came apart in his hand, about eight or ten inches below the handle. "My statement is," he said, cold and hard, "that this thing in my hand is a very specially designed sawed-off shotgun. It will, if fired, blow a hole in Miss Ruysdale about the size of your hat, Chambrun."

"Sit very still, Ruysdale," Chambrun said.

She was motionless. Chambrun sat, cigarette burning between his fingers, smoke curling up, a statue. I felt as if I'd turned to stone myself. We were, I thought, confronted with a madman who was determined to make a five-year dream come true.

"I am going out of here with Miss Ruysdale," Drury said. "If you try to stop me, if you spread any kind of alarm when I'm gone, if you warn Chang, I promise you, you will have lost a very efficient secretary—and a very nice gal from all I've seen of her. I'm sorry to do this to you, Miss Ruysdale, but I can't let five years of preparation go down the drain simply because Mr. Chambrun came up with answers about an hour too soon. Now, if you will stand up and start toward the door—"

"Listen a minute," Chambrun said, without moving. "You must realize that—"

"I don't have time to listen, Mr. Chambrun. You're a nice guy. I know all the things you have to say because you've said them to me as Peter Williams—who is also a nice guy. But you had better damn well play this straight, don't let on, or Miss Ruysdale will pay the price for your zealous protection of that yellow bastard on the twelfth floor."

"I don't care about Chang," Chambrun said. "It's you!"

"I don't care about me, it's Chang," Drury said. "Now move, Miss Ruysdale."

She was looking at Chambrun. She was pale but quite composed. He inclined his head, ever so slightly. She turned and headed for the outer office with Drury directly behind her, his weapon pressed against her back. They were gone, and the door banged shut behind them.

Somehow I got into the action, headed for the phones. "Who first?" I asked. "Wexler? Jerry? Hardy?"

"No one just yet," Chambrun said. "He'll do what he threatened." He brought his fist down on the desk. "I should have known he'd be armed, but I'd seen him searched upstairs by experts!"

"We can't just sit here!" I said.

"Suggest something, Mark," he said, bitter. "We've got just one good chance, and Jerry should have her here in a few moments. When Laura Malone hears he's threatening other lives besides Chang's, innocent lives, she may come down to earth."

There wasn't much point in it, but I walked out through Miss Ruysdale's office to the hall. Between Chambrun's office and mine at the far end of the hall were half a dozen other offices which housed the bookkeeping and accounting for the hotel. There was the bank of four elevators. There was a stairway leading down to the lobby and a fire stair which eventually exited out onto the street level and into the basement. Drury couldn't have taken Miss Ruysdale into the offices, holding a gun on her, or down into the lobby, without starting a riot. That meant the elevators or the fire stairs—up or down.

While I stood there trying to pull my wits together, one of the elevator doors opened and Jerry Dodd appeared with Laura in tow. It turned out Chambrun hadn't lied to her. We had found Drury, God help us. She looked tense and frightened. I didn't say anything, just gestured them into the office.

Chambrun hadn't moved from his desk.

Laura looked quickly around the office and showed instant relief. It didn't last very long.

"Your man has just left here, Miss Malone, holding a sawed-off shotgun on my secretary," Chambrun said. "If we do anything to interfere with him he promises to kill her. In about forty-five minutes General Chang will come down into the public areas. Drury knows that. If I don't warn the FBI and alert my own people, he will make his move at Chang. That will almost certainly be the end for him. If I do pass on the warning someone very precious to me may be blown to pieces."

"Peter Williams?" she asked, her voice unsteady.

"Oh, come on, Miss Malone, let's stop playing games," Chambrun said. "You know as well as I do that the man who's been posing as Peter Williams is your boy. I guessed it. I exposed him. But I didn't think he was crazy enough to be ready to murder anyone who got in his way."

"What do you want me to do, boss?" Jerry asked.

"Listen!" Chambrun said, never taking his eyes off Laura, who was suddenly clinging to the back of a chair for support. "This is all much more elaborate than I'd thought. You were always in on it, Miss Malone. Evidently Tolliver, the agent, is in on it. He sent Mark off to find the phony Peter Williams. That means the real Peter Williams is in on it, too, at least to the point of disappearing so Drury could take his place. Who else, Miss Malone? It is possible that Dr. Coughlin *is* the surgeon who altered Drury's face? Because that much is true; his face has been changed. What about Sam Schwartz—because now we know Tolliver would cover for him? *What is the plan?*"

Laura's whole body was shaking. "He won't hurt Miss Ruysdale," she said. "I know he won't hurt her!"

"You hope!"

"That butcher upstairs can't be allowed to go free," she said, her voice rising. "He has destroyed too many lives. Stay here in your office, Mr. Chambrun; drink your coffee; wait for it to be over and Miss Ruysdale will come back to you unharmed."

"You have all decided that it's all right for you to play God with another human life? I don't care how much of a villain he is, you don't have the right. You ask me to sit here and let him be murdered without lifting a finger to stop it? That makes me a part of your plot. So I have to stop it!"

"You can't risk Miss Ruysdale's life!" I said.

"Miss Malone assures me that he won't harm Ruysdale," Chambrun said, never taking his eyes off Laura. "So I call Wexler and Larch and tell them what's up." He reached for the phone.

"No, Mr. Chambrun!" Laura cried out.

"So you're not sure," Chambrun said. "You're not sure just how mad he is."

She lowered her head. "God help me, I'm not sure," she said.

"Then *what's the plan?*"

Laura straightened up. Her eyes brimming with tears. "He's lived with it for five years," she said. "He's lost his career, his life. He's been hunted by them all that time. Do you understand that? There can never be any peace for him, any security. Chang wins, whatever happens."

"He's already committed a murder," Jerry Dodd said. "He can only burn once. That's why you can't risk Miss Ruysdale, boss."

"He hasn't committed a murder!" Laura said.

"Li Sung," Chambrun said.

"No!" Laura looked at me. "He was with you, Mark, when it happened."

I had been thinking about that and it wasn't so. After our visit from Sung I had left Peter and gone to Chambrun's office to tell him about it. Then we'd gone up to the twelfth floor to look over the arrangements there. I'd gone back down to my rooms then where Peter—or Drury—was waiting. Maybe forty-five minutes in all. It had never occurred to me then that he could have left the apartment, gone up to the roof, murdered a man, and gotten back. Not without help. He was blind!

But he wasn't blind. There was no alibi.

"He could have done it," I said. "There was time."

The little red light on Chambrun's desk blinked and he picked up the phone. "Chambrun here. . . . What? Persuade him to wait . . . because everything isn't kosher down here. . . . Persuade him to wait, god damn it!" He put down the phone. "The General is impatient. He wants to move up his schedule. He wants to start down now." He put both his hands down flat on the desk and leaned forward. "How do we stop this from happening, Miss Malone?" It was so low I could only just hear him.

"I don't know," she said. "My part in it was to disappear so that you would concentrate on finding me. I haven't seen or talked to Neil since then. He was stuck with you."

"Stuck with us, and learning every move we made, every precaution that was being taken to protect the General," Chambrun said. "He even got into the General's suite and saw—we now know—everything there was to see there."

The little red light blinked again. He pushed the squawk-box switch and picked up the phone. We heard Wexler's voice.

"No dice, Chambrun. The General wants to start down now. You're to meet him in the ballroom with your banquet manager. What's not kosher?"

"I think I can identify Drury," Chambrun said. "I need to make sure he isn't on stage when you get downstairs."

"Well, make sure, because we're starting down," Wexler said.

"You have the authority to stop him."

"I wish I knew how to exercise it. Be seeing you."

Chambrun put down the phone and turned once more to Laura. "Will your bloodthirsty boyfriend kill you to get at the General, Miss Malone? Because that's the way it's going to be. He's going to have to kill you and me to get to Chang."

Chambrun had a plan of his own. Wexler couldn't persuade the General to wait, but Chambrun had a way to make him wait. When General Chang and his party of personal guards and the FBI men entered the elevator on the twelfth floor to descend to the lobby, Chambrun was in command. The chief engineer, on orders from Chambrun, stopped the car between floors.

Chambrun, Jerry Dodd and I were down in the lobby when that happened, with Laura in the very tight grip of Jerry's right hand. There was the usual traffic down there, considerably less and more leisurely than it would be at the lunch hour. Mr. Amato, the banquet manager, armed with lists and menus, sweating with anxiety, was trying to get to Chambrun for a consultation before the upcoming get-to-gether with Chang in the ballroom. Chambrun had no time to talk about fresh salmon from the Coast which was or was not on its way. Mr. Amato, unaware of any anxieties but his own, was wounded when Chambrun told him, sharply, that he had no time for him.

"It's a touch-and-go situation," Chambrun said to Jerry and me. "If the General arrives down here ahead of schedule Drury may think I've tipped him. I can't risk that on Ruysdale's account. So the General will have to cool his heels between floors. Jerry, you and Mark will stay here in the lobby. I can see half a dozen of Larch's men. Don't give them any special alerting. It's got to look to Drury as if everything is routine. Miss Malone and I will go up to the tenth floor. At exactly eleven o'clock the engineer will lower the car with Chang in it, and we'll join him. When we come out down here in the lobby Miss Malone and I will be walking directly in front of the General. You will stand by the desk, Mark. If you or Jerry have spotted Drury anywhere, give me the V sign."

"And what then?" Jerry asked.

Chambrun's lips tightened. "Drury will have to cut his way through me and Miss Malone to get to Chang. At that point we play it by ear."

"And if he has Miss Ruysdale with him?"

"God help us all," Chambrun said. "He will be calling the turn then. We'll have to wait and see."

At ten minutes to eleven Chambrun and Laura went up to the tenth floor.

At eight minutes to eleven Miss Ruysdale, looking her customary cool and efficient self, walked into the lobby and came straight toward me where I was positioned at the desk. Jerry, wide-eyed, had seen her and came running.

"It's all over," Miss Ruysdale said, calmly.

"Ruysdale!" Jerry shouted at her. "Boy, am I glad to see you. What happened? Where's Drury?

"Damndest thing," Miss Ruysdale said. "He was taking me up the fire stairs to God knows where. No conversation except an apology for hurrying me. The fire stairs are walled in, you know. I rounded a corner and I never did see what hit me. A man, I think. He gave me a terrific shove and I went toppling over backwards down a whole flight of stairs. Somersaults, no less. God knows why I have no unbroken bone in my body. I heard Drury shout at someone and then, as the saying goes, everything went blank."

"But where is he now?" Jerry asked. He was looking at the elevator indicator on the special car. It was at 10.

"He's in the first-aid room on the ninth floor with one of your men and Dr. Partridge waiting for him to come to," Miss Ruysdale said. "Whoever pushed me knocked Mr. Drury out cold. At best a concussion, at worst a skull fracture according to Dr. Partridge."

"And the other man?"

"I never saw him, Jerry. As I say I tumbled down a flight of stairs to the landing. It must have been a minute or so before I came to and tested my arms and legs to find out if

I was still in one piece. I climbed the stairs and there was Drury, out like a light. I got help."

Jerry let his breath out in a long sigh. "So no fireworks down here," he said. "The boss is on his way." He pointed to the indicator which was coming down, floor by floor. It was exactly eleven o'clock.

I moved toward the elevator, my arm slipped through Miss Ruysdale's. I was feeling a hell of a lot better.

The elevator indicator hit 1. The car door opened. Out came two of Chang's giants flanked by two of Larch's plain-clothes boys. Directly behind them was Chambrun, arm-locked to Laura. And behind them, resplendent in his scarlet trimmed uniform, was General Chang.

Chambrun looked for me where I should have been, at the desk. Then he saw me and Ruysdale. I gave him the okay sign, thumb and forefinger together. His face lit up at the sight of Ruysdale. He turned and said something to Chang and then he and Laura broke out of the protective phalanx and hurried toward us. From the look on his face I could have sworn that there was something more than office memos between him and Miss Ruysdale.

I was watching them so I didn't see the beginning of what was a small commotion behind them. I turned and saw that someone was lying prostrate in front of the General's guards. I guessed that Yuan Yushan had karate-chopped someone else who'd come too close. The guards had drawn their guns and were pointing them at the fallen man. Then another man, ignoring the danger ran forward and knelt beside the fallen man. I recognized Dr. Coughlin.

"Can't you see he's a sick man?" Coughlin shouted at the guards. "Help me move him." I saw it was James Gregory.

It seems to take longer to tell it than the actual time involved. One of Chang's men and one of the FBI boys broke out of the protective formation and lifted Gregory to one side. Coughlin hurried off, I suppose for his medical bag. Chang and company started forward, and all hell broke loose.

Gregory rolled over on his stomach, very much alive. He was holding a Luger pistol in both hands to keep it steady, and he fired, again and again, straight at General Chang's back. The General seemed to leap into the air and then crumpled in a heap on the floor. The Chinese guards turned and opened fire on Gregory. He bounced around like a bundle of rags. People in the lobby were screaming.

The ball game was over—for Chang and for Gregory.

Much later we put most of the pieces together in Chambrun's office. Dr. Coughlin was our chief source of information, and to this day I don't know how much more involved he was than he would admit. Chambrun and Jerry and I, along with Wexler and Miss Ruysdale and a CIA stenographer were present. Laura was in the hotel infirmary, waiting beside a still unconscious Drury.

Some of Coughlin's story was straightforward. He was the surgeon who had performed the operation to change Neil Drury's appearance. That had been three years ago. Drury, a stranger to him though he'd read about him in the papers, had been brought to him by an old friend, a newspaper man named Rattigan—James Gregory Rattigan.

"Rattigan had been stationed in Hong Kong," Coughlin told us. "He'd helped Drury out there to get away from Chang. It cost him his job, and eventually he had to go to the other side of the world because Chang's chums threatened him. He sent Drury to me about that time. He wasn't a criminal trying to escape the law, so I had no reason not to change his face for him. It might save his life because Chang would be endlessly after him. I did it, and so far as I was concerned, that was that.

"A couple of years later Jim Rattigan came back from Europe and came to see me at my clinic. He was a sick man. Emphysema in an advanced stage. He persuaded me to let him stay at the clinic where I could look out for him personally. He was an old friend, I was fond of him, I let him stay.

"About six weeks ago the story broke in the press that General Chang was going to pay a diplomatic visit to this country. Chang was now a big wheel in the government, his revolutionary butcher days forgotten. Not forgotten, however, by Neil Drury and Jim Rattigan."

Coughlin paused to light a cigarette and Miss Ruysdale brought him a Scotch-and-water from the sideboard.

"Drury turned up at the clinic a few days after the Chang story appeared in the newspapers. He and Jim put their heads together. I wasn't in on it, but later Jim told me that they were discussing a plan to 'get' Chang. I told him they were crazy and forgot about it."

That's where I don't know how honest Coughlin was with us, how much he helped. He swore he didn't. But he listened to things he should have told the authorities if he was true-blue Joe.

"There were people willing to help, Drury told Jim," Coughlin said. "There was Peter Williams, who'd been blinded by Chang. There was David Tolliver, Neil's agent, who was willing to help up to a certain point. There was Sam Schwartz, who had been a sort of handyman, dresser, gofor—God knows what for Drury when he was a big wheel in Hollywood."

"But Tolliver told us—" I started to say.

"Of course he told us," Chambrun said. "He was covering

for Schwartz. If we'd checked far enough back on Schwartz in the first place—"

"There was also Drury's girl, his beloved Laura," Coughlin went on. "She was against it, Jim told me, but if Neil insisted on going ahead with it, she'd play along. Neil also thought, in a pinch, they might get help from an old family friend who lived in the Beaumont—a Mrs. Haven. I don't think she ever did more than give Laura shelter for a few hours. Jim couldn't do much to help in his condition, but he'd spent a lot of time drawing up a dossier on Chang on his own account, habits, hobbies, pleasures, friends—the works."

"How did they propose to do it?" Chambrun asked.

"It was pretty sketchy, from what Jim told me. When Chang arrived they would watch him, check his habits and routines. Then they'd pick a time. Laura, and Schwartz, and Tolliver, and the real Peter Williams would create some kind of diversion, some kind of disturbance. Neil, taking advantage of it, would do the job. Then they hit on the idea that Neil would impersonate the real Peter Williams, gain your confidence, be on the inside. It seemed to have worked. Jim, though he was very ill, insisted on coming to the hotel. He wanted to be where the action was.

"Yesterday evening, innocently enough, he got the whim that he wanted to go up to the roof to have a look at the city—maybe his last look. By the wildest kind of coincidence while he was up on the roof, looking at the lights, he found himself face to face with an enemy, a man he had known in China, Li Sung. Li Sung was Chang's man; Li Sung knew that Jim was Drury's friend; as they talked it became apparent that Li Sung guessed Drury was planning something, and now he guessed that Jim was part of it."

"What was Li Sung doing on the roof?" Jerry Dodd asked.

"Chang's advance preparations were very thorough," Coughlin said. "He had found out that Mrs. Haven was an old friend of the Drurys. Sung was scouting out the territory. Well, Jim didn't have much to lose—a few weeks at the most in time. That's really the key to this, gentlemen. He carried a pocket knife. He managed to get it open while he and Sung talked. Sung wasn't afraid of him, a frail invalid. Jim rammed that opened knife into Sung's belly, and in the moment of surprise, managed to topple him over the parapet." Coughlin sighed. "He was committed then. You made things very difficult for them all, Chambrun, by monitoring phones. And brother, you really had me in a spot that first time you came to Jim's suite."

"How so?" Chambrun asked.

"Because Jim wasn't in the next room in bed. He'd gone out to scout around. It was he who warned Schwartz with that 'hit the fan message.' It was he who called his suite while you were there and said they'd found Miss Malone. He had to get you away so he could get back in his room."

"But this morning?"

"It began last night. He began to think Neil shouldn't go through with it. He knew what would happen. Neil had a life to live. And he, Jim Rattigan, didn't. A few weeks at most. But he couldn't get to Drury who was with you people, playing the role of Peter Williams.

"He used the fire stairs to come and go because he didn't want you to know he was circulating. This morning he had decided, not having any particular plan, that he would get to Chang before Neil—probably save Neil his life and his future. He started down the stairs, armed with that Luger pistol, and ran smack into Miss Ruysdale, at the point of Neil's gun. He pushed her aside and let Neil have it with the butt of the gun. Then he came on down to the lobby and waited."

"And you helped him create a diversion," Wexler said.

"I swear to God I had just walked in from the street when I saw him topple over in front of Chang's party," Coughlin said.

I looked at him and I didn't believe him.

"Naturally when I saw those goons pointing guns at him, I ran forward to help him. He was my friend!"

"And when you got him moved aside you ran, in order to be out of the line of fire," Wexler said.

"I ran toward the first-aid room back of the front desk because I knew there was oxygen there! I thought he needed oxygen," Coughlin said.

I heard that and I didn't believe it either. But I guessed he could make it stick.

"What will happen to Neil and Laura and the others?" Coughlin asked.

"They were involved in a conspiracy to commit a murder," Wexler said. "A Federal prosecutor will have to decide what his chances are of proving it."

Chambrun stood up. "Well, gentlemen, I have a hotel to run," he said. He looked at me. "You might go down to the infirmary and see how Drury and Miss Malone are coming along."

I didn't want to go. She didn't know that I was alive, but her hooks were still in me.